# TRAPPED IN THE DESERT

A pair of buzzards circled slowly overhead, aware of the man lying motionless in the rocks but even more aware of the Indians gathered on the cliff top. The midday sun turned the boulders of this unprotected place into a cauldron of simmering heat.

The fugitive flattened himself into the narrow cleft and eased his rifle forward. His canteen was gone, his bay was dead, and the Comanches had him bottled up for the finish. Blood dripping from a gash on his temple, he turned his head, his face tight with concentration. It was too quiet. The Indians were crawling around up there, wondering how best to get at him. He could feel it. They were not fools, and it wouldn't take them long. It was time to do something, even if it was wrong. Beneath him it was a hundred-foot drop to the bottom of the canyon, and retreat was impossible. And even if he could escape, without horse or water in this country a man didn't have much chance.

*It looked like this was the end for Brannigan . . .*

# BRANNIGAN

BY ED NEWSOM

ZEBRA BOOKS

KENSINGTON PUBLISHING CORP.

ZEBRA BOOKS

are published by

KENSINGTON PUBLISHING CORP.
21 East 40th Street
New York, N.Y. 10016

DEDICATED TO MY SONS,

ERNEST, ROBERT AND EDWIN

# ONE

A brassy sky hung over the Barrancas Rojas, a series of sharp basalt cliffs and deep canyons cutting this section of the Texas desert. A pair of buzzards swung in slow circles overhead, aware of the man lying motionless in the rocks, but even more aware of the Indians gathered on the cliff top. The buzzards, wary of that activity, presently gave up and flew away.

It was a wild and lonely land. From the barrancas, the dry country rose eastward to the Guadalupes, north lay New Mexico Territory, south the Rio Grande and the far hills. The man could not see those hills from where he lay, but he knew they were there, as he knew from the town of Dos Brazos Sheriff Dawson and his men would soon come, grim-faced pursuers with ropes in their hands.

Manzanita and catclaw, creosote bush, and even scrub cedar grew upon many of the summits, but there was none on the serrated spine of the highest ridge. The midday sun that beat down turned the boulders of this unprotected place into a cauldron of simmering heat.

The fugitive flattened himself into the narrow cleft and eased his rifle forward. Less than an hour ago, mounted on a fast horse, he had faced south with no aim in his head except flight. A stretch of relatively unobstructed miles lay before him.

The horse could outrun anything that wore hair but couldn't escape a rattler. A bullet was preferable to an agonizing death, but the shot had alerted Indians in the vicinity. They were a hunting party on their way to water, for there was a seep in the area, but until that short time ago, the man hadn't worried about water. The Mexico hills still beckoned, dim blue in the distance. However, now his canteen was gone, the bay was dead, and the Comanches had the rider bottled up for the finish.

He lay in a niche under an overhang, which was hidden from above but overlooked a canyon with sharper cliffs beyond. When the Indians worked around to that lower level across the way, it was the end if he remained where he was, for they would look directly up into his hiding place. They knew these particular crags and would be prepared for every advantage.

Blood dripped from a gash on his temple where a splinter of rock had clipped it. He turned his head and rubbed the blood and grit from his eyes. His shirt was stiff with dried sweat and his broad Irish face, normally creased with good humor, was tight with concentration.

8

A bee buzzed overhead, then sang away into space. It was quiet, too quiet. They were crawling around up there, wondering how best to get at him. He could feel it. Indians were not fools and it wouldn't take them long. He'd dropped two before diving for cover, but there were still three of them left, and it was only a matter of time. Not that Chagro Brannigan had anything against Indians, quite the opposite, but out here it was every man for himself and he'd drawn first blood. They wouldn't be taking that kindly. Redskins all over the Southwest had been crowded, driven, and betrayed, so that anything in a white skin was a foresworn enemy. All they wanted was to get at him.

By now, Dutch and the Seminole were well on their way to the Rio Bravo del Norte and across the river to Camargas, below the border. *I could be a little late,* Chagro thought sourly, *if I get there at all.*

The spot chosen for the strike was a stretch of rough country where, for a matter of several miles, the coach road twisted like a narrow gut between the flanks of rising bluffs and stony hills—an escape route almost impossible to follow. They would follow, of course. Dawson split the posse at this point, half of it to waste precious hours picking up a cold trail. His own trail, better defined, led off at a different angle, but for the length of time it had taken them to fall in behind, his own hadn't been so easy to follow either.

It was the first job, and the last, his share earmarked for a little spread somewhere up in those green hills where a man could settle down and call his inch of earth his own. One of the three, Dutch, the Seminole, or himself, had hung out in Dos Brazos, boozing it up, lying around the cantinas, until they smelled out the lay of the land and knew when the stage from La Playa was due to arrive, what it would be carrying, and who was on the box, all of it.

Everything went well, up to a point. The point was when the shipment did come, it came quietly to allay suspicion and a minor bank official had ridden inside the coach, as though personally escorting his specie was an assurance of its safety. No shotgun guard, no escort. It should have been simple, but when Dutch Gault's fitful and bickering temper suddenly rose, his heavy guns spoke and two men lay dead—the driver and the passenger. Chagro roared his rage at that hair-trigger temper, but the deed was done and too late to undo. So Chagro Brannigan, who had been heard to say that sooner or later a damned fool always outsmarts himself, the happy-go-lucky, hell-for-leather, fiddle-footed Irishman who loved to fight and never bore a grudge, was an outlaw wanted not only for theft but for murder, with every man's hand against him. Because the one who leads must be blamed, his own shoulders would carry the burden of the crime, and therefore he would be hunted as the leader of an outlaw trio.

Thirty thousand was a lot of money to send on ahead, but he'd counted on speed to delay pursuers until the getaway was effective. Thirty thousand. Dutch, he could never be entirely sure about him, but Dutch Gault knew the country well and was a dead shot. The Seminole, Chagro would trust him with all he had anytime or anywhere. He'd saved the Indian's life once and the Seminole never forgot. He had eyes and ears like a fox and would keep the situation in line.

Chagro scrubbed his face again, feeling his belly sweat against the rocks under him. A tight fit, like a lizard. It was stay here and wait until they got the drop on him, or figure something else. There was the posse out of Dos Brazos, good and true men, and Chagro knew most of them, and they wouldn't stand for any nonsense. Then there were the Comanches, his most immediate danger. Somebody else was following too, a lone rider apparently hellbent on catching up, whose dust Chagro had spotted not a mile after leaving the coach road. Yet the Indians were the closest and they were out for the kill. It was time to do something, even if it was wrong.

Inch by inch Chagro pulled himself free of the niche by digging his elbows into the loose talus, until he had a clearer view over the lip of the canyon. It was a better than a hundred foot drop and no way down short of suicide. He stood up carefully, expecting at any moment to feel a bullet or spear from above, but none came. Ahead, the narrowest of ledges, scarcely more than a fissure, ran along the face of the cliff from his hiding place. Retreat was impossible, and anyone on top could draw down on him the minute he showed.

The ledge continued on to a stony outcrop where it petered out in a clump of dry weeds and brush. Chagro was a big man, broad of shoulder, and deep of chest. He carried a rifle, wore a tied-down .44, and over his left shoulder, a bandoleer. He looked around again, then hugged close to the rock face, moved forward, placing each boot carefully before the other.

Loose stones rattled over the edge and bounced and he halted, fresh sweat nettling his body. Two yards, three, to the clump of brush. Here beyond the brush was a defile penetrating the cliff face to the width of a man's body and he backed into it, at the same time, catching a flash of movement among the rocks below. An Indian crouched for a shot.

Chagro flung himself to one side and flipped up his rifle, the blast roaring echoes from canyon wall to canyon wall. The Indian threw up his arms, sagged, and tumbled from sight.

There were no more shots or movement and the silence droned on. Chagro stalled, eyes raking that area across the way, but he found nothing further to arouse his suspicion.

The defile was a dead end and no safer than the spot he had just left. Bitten by a sense of urgency, he moved out again and saw the ledge narrowing before him. Three inches, it couldn't be more than three inches wide, maybe less. Could he stick on that? If he reached a point where it sloped downward, he was in real trouble. He shifted his rifle, wiped his sweaty palms against his thighs to dry them, and then went on.

Something funny about this. There had been only one man across the gorge and no more action from an area where action could be taken. If one, why not more? It could be that the spot, difficult of access, had been risked by only one. In that case, they planned on taking him another way.

The ledge continued, but once again there was an outcrop, a sharp shoulder of stone jutted out from the cliff's face, and beyond that the area widened to a space several yards in diameter and littered with stones. Here the ledge ended abruptly as the cliff fell away to a steep, rubble-littered slope, revealing what had been hidden from sight before—a narrow trail traversing the bottom of the gorge in an "S" shape, its end opening out upon the desert floor in a tumble of boulders. Concealed in this shelter, dismounted, a pair of Comanches would be waiting, for he caught a glimpse of ponies' spotted rumps off to one side in a thicket of mesquite. The Indians knew that these cliffs had only one way out and he'd have to attempt the ledge to escape.

Flattened motionless into the rocks, Chagro studied that dead end. He couldn't go back and couldn't go forward. Descent was out of the question. Trying for a lower position would only bring him into full view of the Indians.

Once, twice on his narrow journey, he'd smelled the brackish odor of water, only faintly, and thus placed the seep on the other side of the gulch. Only one sniper had been sacrificed to that lower level, which bore out his guess that there was too little protection from gunfire from above. They were not prepared to lose any more men and could afford to wait.

Even if escape was possible, without horse or water in this country a man didn't have much chance. Waterholes, seeps, cienagas were few and far between, and given the opportunity, he wouldn't risk this one. Yet there had to be a way.

Three down, which he hoped left only two Indians crouched in the rocks waiting for him to show; eliminating one could even the odds considerably. His own position at the moment was good so long as he remained stationary, but shadows on the cliffs showed it to be around two o'clock. In another half hour, this place would be in the brightest light, another bonus for the redskins.

As he knelt, he swept the stones aside and he hefted one now, testing its weight and balance. With nothing to lose, why not try the simplest trick in the book? As a boy, he'd skipped stones and, like every kid in the land, he knew the flat smooth ones carried farthest.

There was one chance and one only. After some searching, he found what he wanted, and aiming at the point he judged the Indians to be, put all he had into the swing. It landed, gunshots erupted from below, and a bullet struck the cliff and ricocheted with the whine of an angry bee. Another whistled past his head. Briefly a black topknot lifted above the boulders, and Chagro fired and knew he'd hit.

Scrambling over the rocks, the remaining Indian bolted, scooped up his nearest fallen comrade, leaped on a horse, and fled. The other pony reared wildly as he tugged at the reins caught fast in the tough, twisted branches of the mesquite.

Heedless of his footing, Chagro took the talus slope in great, distance-consuming leaps. He fell, rolled, and felt himself pelted, bruised, engulfed in rock, and choking dust. He fell again and rose, then he was down on the level and racing for the horse. The animal, panic-stricken, fought the unfamiliar white man smell, but once aboard, it took no urging to get him going. A yell from a single throat, more like a call, rose to the rear, but Chagro didn't stop.

He pelted south, waterless, saddleless, toward a broken ridge of sand, rubble, and scrub oak, which would offer the nearest shelter. Once lost in those brushy ridges, he would get a breathing spell. By tomorrow afternoon, he'd be suffering for water; he'd have to gamble on the staying powers of the horse.

This one was small and scrawny and barefoot, as were most Indian horses. A veteran of many battles, he bore scars on his shoulders, barrel, and withers, some of the wounds scarcely healed. The bridle and reins were horsehair, greasy with hard use, and he wore a buffalo-gut canteen, the skin worn hard and tough as steel, but empty. There was also a long loop of buffalo hair woven into the animal's mane, by which a galloping rider could hang over one side of his mount's back with only one of his heels showing, enabling him to fire under his horse's neck with maximum protection for himself—a favorite trick of Indians in warfare.

The prints of a barefoot pony, that was the trail he was leaving. How long would it fool the posse?

How long would it fool Dawson?

But as Chagro rode, he suddenly threw back his shaggy head and laughed, a full, free sound; it was the nature of the man that he could laugh.

He hailed originally from the upper San Saba region, which was all Indian territory then. Born Charlemagne Abinidab Brannigan of Irish immigrant parents—a Scripture-roaring father with a fondness for the bottle and a delicate mother who passed to her reward shortly after the boy's birth.

Young Charlemagne Abinidab might have become Abe, save that in no way could his childish lispings manage Abinidab, and his father would accept no less than the full round syllables. Nor did the boy do too well at Charlemagne and thus, despite his father's displeasure, became Chagro. The name stuck.

Before Chagro cut his six-year molars, he was aware that his sire neither wanted nor needed him, so he lit out early, even before he reached his full lanky growth, and worked his way across country and back again. Eventually he grew a large frame padded with an impressive set of muscles, was as strong as a bull, and had a left hook that some said could stop a locomotive. Men liked him, and it was his boast that before the age of seventeen, he had a girl in every town from Kansas to California, which was undoubtedly true. It was also probably true that he could outfight, outcat and outshoot any man on the frontier.

He worked variously as puncher and wrangler, tried his luck at mining on the Yellowstone, uncovered a payable vein, and sold out. Half the profit he lost in a rigged poker game, with the other half, he grubstaked a pair of down-on-the-luck prospectors, neither of whom he ever saw again.

Emerging from the War between the States with the rank of major, he had four decorations for meritorious action under fire, three promotions that he swore he won at blackjack, and more penalties for brawling than any other man in his regiment. The truth was that Chagro Brannigan never could resist a good fight. When the war was over, he shook the red mud of Virginia off his feet and headed West.

At this point, fed up with regimentation, he was ready to join anything so long as it wasn't honest, and it was then he ran afoul of Moseby's Raiders. At first, the daring of it appealed to him, but the raiding just got too thick for a thinkin' man, he said, so he quit them cold. That was the first reason. The second only speeded the proceedings, for it was here he found the Seminole, a keep-to-himself son-of-a-gun that none of the Raiders seemed to take much of a liking to. One thing led to another, and they had the Indian roped to a tree and were doing a beautiful job of carving on him when Chagro stepped in. The Seminole never would be any shakes as a man again, but at least he was alive, which was more than could be said of the half dozen who got in the way.

After that little fracas, a warrant was issued but never carried out because by that time the Raiders' popularity had waned considerably, and several of the members themselves were on the wanted lists. But in the saloons, at the pool tables, and on the open range, wherever men gathered, they still talked of Chagro's exploits. And so the legend grew.

Since then, the honest ones had tried to hire his guns, the law to draft him, the Army to reenlist him, but he managed to walk away from them all without leaving too many enemies behind. Until now.

In particular, Weems. Jefferson Weems, from whom Chagro had lured a woman with no more than a cockeyed grin. Chagro laughed; the hell, he thought, with Weems. Maybe some day he'd go back and see Annabelle. She was a fetching enough female, yes, fetching enough. But there was a Mexican girl down in Camargas—

He turned and scanned his back trail. A dust cloud rolled far distant, which meant pursuit, and no less than he'd expected. He drummed his heels into the pony's ribs and lifted the reins.

# TWO

Seven miles behind Chagro, the posse followed, the men hastily recruited from Dos Brazos and the surrounding countryside. Some were already farther south than they had ever traveled before, the area was unfamiliar, and the chase far from the simple pursuit and capture they had hoped.

It was midafternoon, with barely four good hours of daylight left. The older ones were tired, some of them debating whether to continue or return, for these had homes and families and stock to care for.

Akins was the youngest of this group and the most undecided, but for a different reason. Akins had come against his will, pressured by popular opinion, and now heartily wished himself out of it.

Memory rose clearly and strongly. Billy. He wouldn't have a son today if it weren't for Chagro Brannigan. Snakebit, the boy was. Chagro sucked out the venom and packed the youngster in from the brush where he'd wandered, far gone but alive. Saved his life.

Nor did Akins believe all the stories about Chagro. Those train stickups in Utah were never proven, and how many of the other tales circulated were true? People talked too much. Akins knew from personal experience the aura that could surround a man footloose and fast with his guns. The way most of the others here should understand, even why a man could rob for a stake. Every pilgrim at one time or another had a dream in his head of a spot where the wind blew free, which he could call his own. Half the ranchers in the territory got their start illegally, but they were all respectable citizens now. The two men dead in the coach holdup—well, Akins didn't know about that. A bad break. Disgust for this mission overcame him, and Akins looked around the group. There was no relenting on any of the faces, no mercy at all. Even if the money could be recovered—but why should Chagro let go of it? It would never work, he thought.

"How we know it's Brannigan ahead of us?"

Franks, a former farrier with the Army and now a smith in Dos Brazos, leaned and spat. "It's him all right. That bay's the fastest thing in the country an' he's got a rockin' gait. Ask Tono—he knows."

"Yeah? Even fast hosses run down." It was Jefferson Weems. Weems unscrewed the cap of his canteen and sucked at the water. Drops ran down his chin and he swiped at his chin with the back of his hand.

"If we got to chase him as far as I think we got to

chase him, there's goin' to be a shortage of that," one man said pointedly and gestured to the canteen, "so you better be savin'. The nearest waterhole's over in the east barrancas and nothing more'n a seep. Injuns most always pretty thick around there. We been lucky so far. My notion is we approach that seep pretty cautious."

Weems was a tall, thin man with gimlet eyes and he didn't like advice from anybody. He grunted. "We'll go to it if we got to. Tracks head south, then east, an' they're only barefoot Injun ponies. I don't get it. First we followin' him, then we ain't. We been trailin' since sunup an' no sign of action. Where'd he get to, anyhow? Vanished into thin air."

"Man don't vanish," somebody said. "He's out there somewhere. There's the barrancas—where else would a hunted man go for a layover?"

"Then that's where he'll be expectin' us to look," Weems argued. "He's got to swing south pretty soon so's he can cross the Rio Grande, only he's too cute to lead us in a straight line. He'll beat it down into Mexico. That's where they all go. I look for the trail to swing south. A man like him, Mexico'd be his stampin' ground. Prob'ly holed up there before."

Akins interjected, "From what I hear, the whole country's his stamping ground. Those barrancas are as full of holes as cheese. Or he could be a thousand other places. The coach was hit yesterday morning and this is today. Figure he didn't sit around pickin' his teeth while the night wasted away."

21

Weems whipped around at once, his bearded cheeks twisted in a snarl. "What's the matter, you want out? Expect somebody else to do your dirty work for you? You got as much in this as I have. He's a sneak thief, an' a murderer. We'll catch him because we're goin' to head him off before he gets to the river."

Akins's smooth cheeks settled, his eyes narrowing beneath the wide brim of his hat. Weems's knuckles were barked. Was that from beating his wife? Akins glanced up at the sky, the west bathed in saffron light, the long shadows already lying across the desert floor. A year out of Ohio and already the richest man in Dos Brazos, Weems didn't know anything outside of Dos Brazos. He didn't know Chagro Brannigan either to make a prediction like that. There were dozens of little Mexican villages, not only across the Rio Grande but the Brazos, the Bravo and the Nueces, and all along further south. Barring accidents, Chagro was as good as home free right now.

Weems growled, "Brannigan's gone too far this time an' he'll pay with his neck. He's got away with too much too long an' I want him to swing. I'll pull the rope myself to see the job's done proper. He's ahead of us all right, I smell him like I'd smell a curly wolf."

"Thought this was strictly business with you," Akins said. "Sounds like you got a personal axe to grind."

Franks looked at Weems, Freeman, Akins, Dawson. Tono looked at Weems. "Maybe I have!" Weems snapped. A moment later he pointed.

"How about that, Tono?"

The one called Tono shrugged. He was a squat, pock-faced, half Ute half Caddo-Comanche, the best tracker in the district, and he did not like Weems. He had nothing against the fugitive except a duty to run him down, but the man's cleverness baffled and outraged him. There were few legible tracks so far. Doubling back, circling, and in many places lost entirely.

The scout's keen eyes had been scanning the earth, tracing faint scars almost invisible, which now became sharply visible but crossed and recrossed to deliberately confuse pursuers. For a time this last maneuver had puzzled Tono, but he was puzzled no longer.

"White man horse. Indian pony too, five Indian pony. Them no hurry. Hunt, I think. In no hurry. See? White man come after. One no see the other. Pretty close, maybe. Then somebody else, he come, crisscross. Like so." Tono made a cross with his wrists, turning back to indicate where a second traveler, another shod horse, had entered the picture. The Indians, then a white man, and after that, a second white man raveling out the first white man's trail. *"You* read," he suggested to Weems. "Clear there on ground, huh?"

"Don't get snotty," Weems snapped. "You point, that's all you're here for."

There was no further comment and the group rode some distance without speaking. The scrape of hooves against the dry earth and the creak of saddle leather, broken occasionally by a muttered exclamation, were the only sounds to be heard.

Once a coyote broke cover, then faded again like a shadow into the scrub juniper.

The first of the barrancas loomed off to the left and the trail swung. They were traveling due south now. Up ahead, Tono suddenly halted, rising in his stirrups.

"Something over there. Dead, I think. Many buzzards." He searched the area carefully, but there was no sign of life anywhere. He set spurs to his mount and the others pelted after him. The birds flew up in a cloud as the men approached.

Weems rode up, panting. "His horse—it's the bay! Boys, we got him now! How far can he go without his horse? He's up in those rocks somewhere."

Freeman looked around narrowly. "That's right. Probably with a rifle trained down on us right now."

"Not a chance. No place to hide this side, or the summit either. Bare's a church."

"A trail, though. You can just see it, real faint."

Dawson, Akins, and Weems got down, examining the carcass. The Indian walked carefully around it, then, with his inspection complete, got back on his horse. The bay's body was bloated, its eye sockets emptied clean by buzzards, and ragged holes ripped in the skin by talons and beaks, but the animal also bore a bullet hole straight between the eyes. The slug had entered the brain and death was instantaneous. None of the stiffly outthrust legs were broken, there was no sign of injury other than that made by the bullet hole. Diamondbacks walked quietly and gave little warning,

24

Tono knew.

Much could be learned about a man when you trailed him, how hard he pushed his mount, the length of time he allowed the animal to rest, the time he gave it to graze from the size and frequency of the droppings. Tono began to feel a grudging respect for this Chagro Brannigan, and a curiosity. Brannigan hadn't crowded the bay but allowed it to conserve its strength for a fast push, if needed. Whenever possible, he had kept to the stony areas rather than sand, not only to leave no clear trail but for easier travel for the horse. Brannigan hadn't known about that other rider following him, for nowhere on the trail had there been any indication of a meeting. The Indian glanced up at the towering rock. Chagro Brannigan had soon known about the Comanches, though.

"I'm goin' up." It was Weems again.

There was an explosion of dissent.

"You're crazy," Freeman snapped. "If you go up, you go alone. It's coming dark. I hear he's pretty good with guns and if he's up there, I'm not sticking my head in any noose. If not, he won't go far without a horse. We can pick up his trail easy in the morning. Time enough to do what's to be done come daylight."

Franks hesitated. Chagro wouldn't be up there anyway. He wouldn't have sat idly in those rocks because he couldn't find a way down. Not Chagro Brannigan. Still, they would have to have their search; nobody would be satisfied without a search.

Franks had had little to say, but seeing no

25

immediate hope of returning to town, shrugged and agreed. "He's right, boys. There's a trail down the middle of this pile, but nobody could reach it from above. There's this way in an' only one way out an' that's by the trail at the far end. The other cliff's real steep to where the water is. If he's in there, we got him bottled up." Franks looked around at the others, having no stomach for any of this. Like many another law-abiding citizen, he preferred to go about his business quietly, maintaining home and fireside, seeing his children grow up happy and carefree, lying comfortably beside his wife after a hard day's work. He said, "I guess we can get us some cover under that overhang an' camp right here if we got to. How you figger, Tono, all right to camp here?"

But the Indian was gone in his silent, catfooted way. Presently he came back but had nothing more to say.

It took four laborious hours the next morning to search out the ridge. They found empty shell casings on top, blood where apparently a Comanche had died but no body, for his companions would have lugged him off, and a few drops of blood in the niche. For the rest it was a puzzle. No man could get out unless he backtracked and went over the top, or backtracked and took the trail at the bottom of the gulch. Evidence pointed to the fact that Chagro had done neither. Short of sprouting wings and flying out, how had he escaped? There had been a fight, some kind of a fight, there were tracks of unshod ponies in the mesquite below and pony tracks where two riders had left in a hurry. Otherwise, nothing.

Weems was hot and frustration goaded him to fury. "We covered damn near every inch of them rocks. So what's next?"

"Get on with it," sourly retorted Freeman. A strange, reticent man, slim as a rattler, with cold pale eyes and a livid scar, not too well healed, on his right cheek. Nobody knew much about Freeman, he'd appeared in town a few months ago, laid around, did some gambling. He was close-mouthed; no one knew how he lived, but everybody figured he had a past somewhere and was only waiting for something good to turn up. When he swung his head, the long scar on his cheek showed clearly. He'd have no hesitation at shooting a man down, but it was plain he was tired of Weems' bellyaching. "Where there's water we fill our canteens. There's no Indians around now to be scared of, I'll guarantee that."

It was a stiff climb, a narrow trail twisting fifty feet nearly straight up to a heap of boulders and around a shelf to a small pocket beneath a ledge. Here water slowly trickled down a rock slab into a small depression, the liquid collected there tepid and green with scum.

Sheriff Dawson was a fat man and he'd already shed a pound of sweat. He leaned, and swore. "Stinks."

"Sure," Akins said cheerfully, "but a dry spring and it's this or nothing. Forty miles to the nearest waterhole." Akins unscrewed the cap of his canteen and the others followed suit. Franks grunted his reluctance as they followed the trail

27

down. Akins poured water into the crown of his hat and offered it to his mount, which drank thirstily.

Dawson remained sitting on a rock. Still puffing from the first climb, he finally heaved to his feet.

"The horses the Indians get up there to water must be half goat," Franks said on the second trip. Akins shrugged. The job finished, Akins swung to saddle and fell into line.

"A single Injun on a barefoot horse ahead of us. What we followin' a single Injun for?" Weems demanded. He glared at Tono. "For my money Chagro Brannigan's still back there somewhere, holed up in those cliffs. We could have missed him. We trailed him that far, didn't we? How much farther could he get without a horse? I don't see no more tracks like he could have made." Weems swung again, pinning the sly humor on Tono's face. Weems edged close, his own face ugly.

"You leadin' us into somethin'? I don't know you. I don't trust you neither. Not the way you look. Like you was laughin' up your sleeve. If you know somethin', you better spit it out, redskin, or I'll—"

"Shut up, Weems." Dawson turned his leonine head and eyed the other coldly. "What's the matter with you? You been needlin' since this trip began. Our man's ahead of us. He's got to be. You figger it out. His tracks in, blood on the rocks an' cartridge cases, ground all chewed up from Injun ponies. One lit out of here streakin' east—there's a Comanche camp over in those hills somewhere,

28

an' the other in the opposite direction—the direction a outlaw would go for escape. I still don't know how he done it, but my guess Chagro Brannigan got away on an Injun horse an' that's his tracks."

Weems cursed and blustered but quieted.

Sheriff Dawson too was irritated by Tono's attitude, yet he was well aware that without him this bunch wouldn't have gotten far. Akins wasn't too anxious; Freeman, a restless one strictly out for blood, anybody's blood, but he was no tracker; Franks, a family man whose wife was expecting and who consequently spent his time looking back. But Dawson had seen a brown hand hover over a knife hilt, saw the black eyes measuring Weems for six feet of Texas earth, and knew it was no time for hesitation.

A self-styled, strong exponent of law and order, Dawson nevertheless sought the safe side, preferring to maneuver others to do his chores, yet claiming the glory for his own. Elected a year ago by popular vote from a field of no candidates, he'd managed to retain his seat because there had been no moot questions to settle. Now with thirty thousand of the bank's money gone and two men dead, as sheriff he was forced to the wall. It was either charge out and play the role or find some plausible means of exit. Secretly all Dawson wanted was for somebody other than himself to lay hands on the culprit, string him up, and be done with it. For more than one reason, the sheriff of Dos Brazos had no patience with owlhoots. But when Chagro Brannigan, of whom he had heard much, and two strangers, of whom he had heard nothing at all, showed up in town, he'd had the unpleasant feeling of shoals ahead. Never seen together, the two were easy to spot—one, a big beef with a mean eye, and a tall, skinny Indian. Not local, some other breed. And Chagro Brannigan.

Dawson turned and looked back. "I ain't too happy for us to be in this position if there was somebody up above," he remarked. "With a rifle they could pick us off like sitting ducks."

At that moment there was a sharp report, followed by the whine of a bullet. Akins rolled from his horse and all scattered for cover.

# THREE

No more shots came. Belly down in the dirt behind the shelter of a round boulder, Dawson raised his head cautiously.

"What the hell—?" But the rocks presented a blank face, there was no sign of the sniper, and the silence droned on.

"Bad news," Akins whispered off to his left. "He's got us pinned here as long as he wants us."

Twenty yards away and nearest the cliffs, the Indian rose on one knee, paused to measure the distance, then keeping to a crouch, sprinted for the protection of the overhang. Nothing happened. Yet a moment later when Freeman shifted position, a bullet kicked up rock not six inches from his foot.

"He could of got us before," Freeman snarled. "What's he want us for now?" Freeman's face was ugly and his voice was tight.

Freeman got his answer direct, the speaker bitterly sweating it out and thinking of his wife.

"He didn't want us then. Plain enough, ain't it? Now we're out in the open, he plans to pot each one of us until we're all finished. Who's gonna pull the chunk outta this fire?"

"Tono," muttered Akins, "but he's the only one that can get away," and he eased his elbows from the hard ground.

"I'm goin' to have pint-sized rocks printed on my rear," Dawson complained. "This ain't exactly a feather bed. If he don't panic the horses—" Akins turned his head to answer when the rifle cracked and Dawson's horse reared, wavered, then plunged to his knees. He gave a couple of kicks, then rolled over, dead. Another shot exploded the canteen.

Dawson yelled, the yell subsided to a groan. "My God! What'd he do that for? Target practice! He don't mean to leave us anything."

"One down," almost wept Franks. "This is the way it's goin' to go an' we'll never get out of here."

Tono had halted again, searching the ridge from his new position. For a long moment he crouched, then was snapping up his weapon to fire when the fourth bullet came. Fifty yards away his mount jerked violently, jumped aside, then stood trembling, ground-hitched by the reins dangling to earth. The animal wasn't hit, but water ran from the canteen looped to the saddle horn, ran freely, then died to a trickle.

The Indian sent a shot upward and the bullet chipped the rock face. The sheriff squeezed off his own follow-up, which went wild. A rifle sprang from a slightly different section of the ridge and another horse screamed protest as still another canteen exploded, losing its contents in one mighty geyser.

Behind his rock Akins frowned. Something real odd about this. He raised his chin and stared upward at the cliffs, seeing no space there to hide a man, no movement of any kind to indicate human presence. Yet the rifleshots had come from above. He had to be up there. *Who had to be up there?* Akins too had evaluated those covering tracks and now felt a leap of traitorous elation at the possibilities.

Somebody—a friend of Chagro's it had to be—was fighting a delaying action. He wasn't after the horses but the canteens. Dawson's horse was a mistake. Akins doubted the rifleman wanted the members of the posse individually or he'd have picked them off before. Collectively, he meant to delay the pursuit. For how long?

No further explosions erupted from the rocks and the heat-shimmered air was as still as death. Whoever manned the gun was a superb shot, his marksmanship incredibly precise, despite that first accident, and the same fear for the moment was in each of the watchers. With facility like this, a man's skull could erupt far more readily than any object of leather and metal.

Freeman raised a hand and wiped his thin cheeks. "Like to get one good crack at him. Just one. Maybe it's Brannigan after all. Maybe it is him."

"Hang around long enough, we'll find out," Franks growled. Akins and Dawson forebore to reply. Weems was cursing steadily into the sand but didn't raise his head. The Indian Tono was gone, faded around the cliff face and out of sight.

Crash! Another canteen. The horse screamed, rose on its hind legs, and bolted away.

"Sonofagun just makin' fun of us," snarled Weems. "None of the rest of you got the guts. I'm half a mind to go up there after him myself."

"You do that," advised Dawson and eased his heavy body to a different position behind the boulders. Sweat was running in rivulets down his fat cheeks and his face had a pinched look.

Tono showed again briefly, then once more vanished from sight. A hell of a lot of good he was doing, thought Freeman. The trip wasn't worth it, not running into something like this. A sweet fix, the posse pinned down in the rocks with the only free water between here and forty miles running out on the ground before their eyes. *One, two, three*. No, *four*. Another sharp report and his own mount jerked about, shoulder stung, then with the horse in exactly the proper position, there was a second blast and the canteen whipped wildly as its contents let go.

Freeman, thin lips twisted with rage, snaked his gun free of the holster and lifted the muzzle. But he didn't fire. It was out of range and he knew it.

Akins looked on in near contempt. He was no grandstander himself, but for a cool one Freeman had jumped a mile when it came his turn.

Weems shoved his hat above the rocks; a swift answer from above carried the hat ten feet away.

"Notional, ain't he? Shoots who he feels like shootin' at."

Notional. Like a playful kid. The sniper must have seen the Indian yet let him go. Why? He'd missed Freeman by inches but only because he wanted to and in the way he wanted to. The fun with Weems's hat. There was no sense to it, no pattern such as a man with deliberate intent would use. It wasn't only delaying action, Akins decided, it was humor, too. If it was a kid, he was good, the best Akins had ever seen.

Tono was back; he had caught the horse and the animal was tethered nearby out of sight. The Indian shrugged and spread his hands. Obviously escape was possible so long as the rifleman remained where he was, and if the other five could manage to reach the overhang. Then by keeping the barranca for cover—

It was too long a chance. An hour passed, the sun began to sink, and the shadows grew long. Sweet, hot sage smell rolled along the ground and the horse stamped restlessly over by the cliff.

"We wait till dark before we pull out," Dawson said, "we can't do nothin' else," and added with a show of bitterness, "More time wasted. This trip's been jinxed from the start. Somebody out there's smarter than us, that's all. Anybody of the notion to turn back? There's another day comin'."

"Not me. I aim to see the bastard hang—I said it before." Weems pulled out a plug of tobacco and bit off a chew.

"You must want him pretty bad."

"I do!"

"What for?" Akins shot back but thought he knew. A slim, coaxin' woman with a sharp pair of

35

eyes—had they crossed Chagro Brannigan? The Irishman could charm the bees off a stump.

"We goin' without no water?" Weems presently said. "He got near all of it. Six men an' one canteen. I wonder how the rest of the posse is doin'?"

Franks had only one weary comment. "Why worry about them? We got troubles enough of our own."

A cardinal chirped from the top of the cliff and burst into song, another fluttered down from her nest nearby. Traveling close to the earth, men learned to read its creatures: the raucous cry of a jay, suddenly silenced, a rabbit's frightened spurt of movement, the abrupt cessation of a small bird sound. The cardinal pair had emerged from hiding and were splitting their throats on the cliff top. The birds were the best indication in the world that nobody was around. Whoever was up in those rocks had had his fun and left.

"Quiet now," Freeman muttered.

"Yeah." They lay still for a time further, then Dawson heaved to his feet and picked up his rifle. "Guess it's safe. I'd say he's gone." All was still.

"Well," Dawson said, "one thing, we're not chancin' that seep. It's goin' to be a long trip otherwise an' one of us has got to ride double. Franks, I'm of the opinion your place is home. You oughtta go back. Akins, how about you?"

"Carrie's a practical woman. I'll stick."

"All right. Anybody else? I'll see the price of a thousand is put on his head, fifteen hundred for all three. Dos Brazos can raise that."

Freeman turned, catlike, he'd seemed to wait for this. "I'll go."

The Indian's black gaze shifted to Weems, then his shoulders moved. "I go," he decided.

Dawson hesitated, looking around. Akins was the steadiest here and the most responsible. Let Akins take the risk. Younger, too. There was a limit to belly crawling and forty blistering waterless miles held no allure, even if Chagro Brannigan was at the end of it. With the right maneuvering, his sheriff's position in the town could remain secure; as its elected official, the sheriff had the privilege to delegate authority as he saw fit. He took a deep breath and it caught; he'd felt part of something drain from him.

"You don't look so good," somebody said.

"Don't feel so good." Dawson was not feigning this. "Maybe I'll feel better when I rest awhile." He straightened slowly.

They stared at him. "Maybe you better not go," somebody else said. "We won't be slowin' any once we get on the way. Think you can make it?"

"I don't know." Dawson spoke wearily though color was beginning to return to his face. "I had these things come on me before but not so hard. I *got* to go, me bein' sheriff an' all. But I dunno—" He sighed again and shook his head. "Guess you're right. Akins, you can take over. I'm makin' you a deputy."

"Me? Nothing doing!" Akins retorted but Dawson waved a hand.

"You're capable. Fam'ly can get along without you for awhile, you said it yourself. You take

37

charge. Well, what do you know? I just happen to have a star here in my pocket. Stand still—"

Akins had stepped back, then stood; he would have protested for what good it did. "There. Now you're duly deputized. I want Brannigan an' the two others in it with him an' I want that money. It's up to you. Understand? Bring 'em in."

The effort seemed to have exhausted him. He walked slowly toward Franks's horse, Franks had to help him onto the saddle, then Franks climbed up behind. Akins knew the sheriff and was inclined to suspect trickery, but he knew also that this was not the case.

He watched Dawson ride away, Franks sticking double. Dawson didn't look back.

"Takes more'n a star to make the law," Weems observed nastily.

Akins did not reply. An easygoing man, he was seldom ruffled, kept his own counsel, and rarely showed his feelings. When he did get angry, his voice became soft; it was one whisper above a purr as he spoke to Weems.

"If you're going with me, let's move."

Tono was laughing, a half grin out of one side of his mouth. Nice congenial bunch, all brothers under the skin. Akins thought ahead to the trail, to Chagro Brannigan, to this manhunt that was something he'd wanted no part of from the start. He spat, his mouth tasted bad.

"Hell," he swore. He still felt tricked.

# FOUR

In a curve of hills west and south of the Guadalupes, there is a pass used by generations of travelers seeking to avoid the longer route to Mexico. The pass is for the wayfarer who fears not to leave a trail, nor would himself seek to remain hidden.

To the left of that curve of hills some four miles as the crow flies, there is to be found a series of undulating lava ridges that extend far outward into the thickets of ironwood and mesquite on the desert floor. Not a half mile east of this point is a particular lava ridge, not so high but sharper than the others, whose jagged teeth gnaw at the sky. And herein is a certain notch where, it is said, if one has knowledge of it and stands on the flatland below to sight carefully through this notch, he may catch a glimpse of a secret trail over the lava beds. If he follows this trail, it will lead him to a mesa and, in a pocket of rocks, a spring. It is a spot known only to a very few and from it one has a clear view all around.

Chagro had struck into the very heart of the desert country, and this now was country he knew.

It was also country the Indians knew. Not only of the notch but of the water as well, for they were born to the land and nurtured by it, and since to them it meant life or death, there was little of that land that was not an open book to them.

Chagro was well aware of this and of the need to exercise the utmost caution, for he had no intention of exchanging a noose for a slit throat and the loss of his hair, if he could help it.

One advantage was the barefoot pony. A man's leather footgear identified him as surely as his shod horse; these things they recognized right away, as they would accept, perhaps with only a little curiosity, prints the same as their own. Thus when it became necessary to walk, Chagro did so with the greatest care and whenever possible, where no prints of his boots would be left.

He had turned at right angles and headed west, then south again to lose himself in a forest of scrub oak. Here he rested the horse, then went on. So by traveling like a Comanche, keeping the brush for cover, riding slower so no dust would rise, he reached the ridge. It was traveling such as he'd done before and he didn't mind that, except he was impatient due to the few miles covered.

Late that afternoon, he put the wiry, little animal to the draw that led up into the lava hills, stopping often to look and listen. Nearing the summit he turned sharp left, traveled through a stand of juniper, climbed another short rise, and found the spring.

The water was cold and clear, welling up from some deep underground source. The black stone underfoot was worn smooth from use, and on the rocks overhead and beside the water, ancient pictographs depicted the Indians' life of long ago, not much changed from today—hunting, warfare, the gathering of food.

Chagro watered the pony, drank quickly himself, filled the canteen and backed away at once, descending to the spot earlier chosen for its seclusion.

He stood for some time studying that empty land spread out below. Nobody following, nothing at all. Four hours after leaving the barranca he had spotted smokes, but he was too far away for those particular smokes to mean anything here. Where was the posse? It should be coming along, at least some of it, for Dawson would have split the group, part to take his trail, the remainder to go after Dutch Gault and the Seminole. Somewhere the two sections would meet to compare notes, which was no concern of his if he could keep enough leaps ahead.

It wasn't working out too badly. Dust, heat, and flight was the route he'd chosen and if he sometimes wondered what had been in his head to undertake such a thing, he had nobody to blame but himself. The money in itself meant little, he would have given all that away, but it was too late to turn back. Besides, there wasn't only himself. A chuckle escaped him. Ten thousand dollars in the offing and a belly caved to the backbone from hunger. Would the money really buy peace in that green haven as he'd thought? Or would he ever actually see it? He couldn't be arrested down in Mexico, but the man who lived by the gun usually died by it.

He sat down with his back to a rock and closed his eyes, knowing he would sleep, and with a sense sharpened by years of alertness, for how long that sleep would last.

When the sun touched his face he woke swiftly, his hand on his gun and all his senses aware, within the time allotted. Perhaps no more than a half hour, yet he felt rested. Again he scanned the distance. The sun was lower and shadows began to creep into the hollows and the air was cooler. A cricket emerged from the dry leaves at his feet and began to chirp, another answering a few feet away. The pony, tremendously invigorated by the life-giving water, cropped the dry grass that grew along the fissures in the lava.

Chagro pulled papers and tobacco from his pocket and built a smoke, eyes still searching all that dry and empty terrain. He was uneasy without knowing why—he watched the horse. Placid, still cropping grass. He ground out his smoke and rose. This place was beginning to feel unhealthy; at dusk he'd start out. Only common wisdom kept him from taking flight now.

There was a cluster of brush and broken rock behind him and he climbed to this higher vantage point, blended into the shadows, and again searched the area all around.

And then he saw it, a speck on the horizon. The

speck grew, took shape, and became a single rider on a black horse, but still too far away to make out any details except that the rider was really fanning it. Somebody wanting to get some place in a big hurry. And not being pursued? The traveler was alone in the vast emptiness of space. Once the animal faltered but regained its stride and plunged on.

Chagro swore. He got the pony and quickly moved back farther into the brush, secured him and scrubbed out the tracks with a whip of mesquite. Then waited. The rider was still coming and headed this way. A *woman?* What was a woman doing out here? Riding like the devil was after her, she'd pushed the horse to the limit and blobs of white lather streaked its shoulders and flanks.

She was near the edge of the lava when the black stumbled and went to its knees, throwing her heavily to the sand. And up on his ledge, Chagro gritted his teeth and lowered his rifle. The black struggled to its feet and stood with sides heaving. He looked at the horse sharply.

"Damn crazy female," Chagro muttered, and with rifle in hand, he went down. He knew as soon as he came close who she was and shock got into him and turned him wary. Annabelle Weems. Carroty red hair hanging in wisps about her face, shaken by the fall but unhurt. She rolled over and sat up as he approached.

He lifted her to her feet, steadied her, then stepped back. "I don't believe this! What the hell are you doing here? And what are you trying to do to that horse—kill him?"

Her face was dusty and sweat streaks furrowed the dust but she shrugged. "I was tired of that grubby little Dos Brazos. I wanted to get away, so I came."

There was more to it than that and he'd find out what. But not now. Her trail had wound up here. And out in the open like this—

"Come on," he said gruffly, caught up the black's reins and with the woman moved back up the lava to a spot he'd earlier rested.

He left her sitting on a rock, removed saddle, pack, canteen, and bedroll from the horse, leaving only the bridle. Afterwards he rubbed the animal down with a clutch of leaves and twigs until he cooled, then led him to water, allowing him to drink only sparingly, and tethered him nearby.

The pack was open on the ground and she was sitting waiting for him to kindle a fire. "No fire," he said curtly.

"But I brought food!"

"Forget it," he said. He hunkered down, staring at her. "Now I want some answers. I thought I'd picked a good hiding place." And although he knew, he asked, "How'd you find me?"

She shrugged and shoved back her hair impatiently as though irritated at his lack of comprehension. "I didn't try to. I just took the best horse and started out. I heard about the stagecoach and left before the posse. Nobody in the posse knows I'm gone and won't until they get back. Everybody knew you'd go to Mexico. So I thought if I rode hard enough, you'd find me."

"Not right at all. You had nothing to do with it. That horse's got more sense than you have—he was after water. Smelled it, and it's my guess he's been here before. You're carrying a canteen, did it ever occur to you to find some way to get a little water to him? That if I'd gone on as I wanted to do, you'd have probably died on the desert? Just to strike out like that—Good God! You know I can't take you back."

She showed sudden temper at that. "I wouldn't go back! I'll never go back. I'm going with you."

"Yeah?" Chagro growled. How she'd made it this far he'd never know. The posse, the Indians— "Look," he said. "It's high time we got some things straight. I don't want you with me, understand? I'm on the run and I travel best alone. I didn't ask you here and you'd only be in my way." Then he stopped. What could he do, *make* her go back? How? Chagro felt crowded, boxed in, and rebellious. How had he ever thought this woman pretty? She wasn't even alluring, she was just one damned big headache. A liability. And she wanted to tag along clear to Mexico!

She was about to tip over with exhaustion, he saw, but not too tired to bat her eyes at him. Well, it had worked before. That eye was faintly black and one cheek discolored under the dust. What kind of donnybrook had she been in?

"You looked at me once, what's the matter now?"

She couldn't understand that a chase wasn't a chase when it squatted on your doorstep. That girl in Camargas was looking better all the time.

"Don't ask questions, all right? I'm trying to figure out what to do with you. This is no affair for a woman to be mixed up in. You had no business coming in the first place. You didn't seem to mind Dos Brazos before, what set you off?"

Her small pointed face settled and grew hard, her lips thinned witchlike as her chin seemed to sharpen, and he had an unexpected picture of the Annabelle of ten years hence. Taut and needle-nosed and determined. A woman like that would run the world or try to, with melted hell in the teepee from morning to night. If it came time for a man to tie unto himself a mate, God help the man who tied this one.

"Jefferson. You might know! He's a pig—a dirty pig. I never want to see him again!" Annabelle sniffed. "Shoving people around, thinks he's God. Well, I got tired of it and that grubby little place. It's none of his business what I do, I don't care what he says."

Chagro had the sense of treading very lightly. "He got some hold over you?"

She shrugged again; she seemed to have spent all the subject she desired and was brief to the point of rudeness. She'd come out from Iowa to marry Jefferson Weems and he wasn't what she expected. But he was the richest one around and a woman had to have a man in this country, didn't she? But she'd got sick of him and left.

"You mean you're his *wife?*" Chagro exploded. "If you were a man, I'd wring your neck! Your husband's out there gunning for me and, by God, if I don't feel he's got a right. Look—I never

46

fiddled with a married woman in my life and don't aim to start now, much less run off with one!''

Annabelle's lips curled. "I wasn't a married woman when I saw you. I married him after. Anyway, don't tell me you're so fussy! You're the kind that'd have a different woman every night. You can't fool me!''

"Oh, for Christ's sake," Chagro said and rose. "So you've left him for good, or so you say. Kind of sudden, wasn't it?''

She got to her feet and came toward him, touching his shoulders, his chest, once more all melting sweetness and purring invitation. "Can't you guess the reason?''

He grunted. "I didn't plan on anything like this. You're dynamite. Why couldn't you stay back where you belong and leave me out of it? I told you I travel light and I travel fast. I'm a fugitive—a hunted man. You taggin' along will make it rough, so don't complicate things.''

"Then that means I can go with you.''

He turned, said over his shoulder, "I'll take you to a village across the river and you can tie up with somebody traveling back from there or whatever else you want to do. If we get out of this alive—and there's a good chance we won't—you go your way and I'll go mine. I wash my hands of it.''

She brushed aside his words and looked around. "Aren't we going to spend the night here?''

"No.''

"But I'm tired! Where's the money?''

His eyes narrowed under his hatbrim. "What

47

money? Maybe I'm carrying it in my sock. I haven't got any money."

"Somebody has."

Chagro clamped his lips tight and went on about his business. He untied and watered the pony, did the same for the black, and saddled him. Dusk had fallen and bushes and trees bulked dark against the desert floor. Temper gouged him but he held it down. He'd like to throttle her! Nobody would believe the whole thing wasn't his idea.

"But why can't we sleep for awhile? There's nobody around."

"Lady," he said, thoroughly out of patience, "if you travel with me, we go when I say go. Understood?"

Her lip thrust out but she said nothing more. He picked up her pack, the bedroll and lashed them on the black, his mind racing ahead to the possibilities, the danger. The possibilities held insufficient appeal and the danger was very imminent. Once more he was in a bind. So far as Jefferson Weems was concerned, Chagro hated his guts, but that didn't alter the fact that this woman was his wife. It was pure charmed luck she'd made it this far and not a chance in the world she'd make it back. There'd been Indians once and she hid in the rocks until they passed. They hadn't seen her.

She watched Chagro now as she idly poked a stick at a crack in the lava. "There was somebody else, too," she said. "A rider on a pink horse—yes, pink. He seemed to blend with the desert. Well, pale tan then. You know the color."

Chagro didn't. A young man, she thought, it

was a large young man, wearing a wide hat and at a distance, so she couldn't tell much, really. He was by himself, not with the Indians, and for awhile she'd thought he was following her. Her husband was a devil, she reiterated, and it would serve him right if she never went back to Dos Brazos.

"Let's go," Chagro said curtly.

She moved so slowly he had the urge to give a grab and heave her aboard. "You're not as nice as I thought you'd be."

"I'm alive," Chagro said significantly, "yet," and swung to the pony. At that moment a shot rang out, another, and at the second bullet, the black grunted and swayed. "Watch it!" Chagro yelled, flung his rifle to his left hand, and leaped for her even as the black dropped. Chagro pulled the woman down with him, hit the ground, and rolled over and over, coming to rest in a thicket of mesquite and boulders.

"Who is it?" she whispered. He felt her trembling beneath him.

"Can't tell yet. Indians, most likely. Just lie quiet."

"Will they kill the other horse? If they shoot the pony, we can't get out of here!"

"Shut *up!*" This was insufficient cover at best and she'd give their position away with her yammering. It was Indians, he could smell them. Something moved in the brush but he couldn't see what it was. A jackrabbit streaked past, going like his tail was afire. The pony tramped nervously and whinnied in alarm. They were out there all right and not far away.

Minutes passed. Chagro raised his head slowly, saw nothing in the near dark, heard nothing anywhere about, yet he had the feeling of being watched. A sliver of moon slowly lifted in the east, casting a pale glow on the sand. Rock and mesquite were only vague shadows and all was still, as still as the grave.

The black was dead, he'd kicked convulsively a few times and that was it. Annabelle began to whimper. "I'm afraid! They're going to get us, I know they are! And I've heard what Indians do to women—"

Chagro raised on one elbow, measuring for the point of her jaw, telegraphing that intent; her eyes grew large but she subsided. And then he looked up. Four Indians loomed against the western skyline's fading light and they were coming in. Chagro whipped his rifle around and the slug caught the foremost in the face even as he leaped; the yell died in his throat.

A bullet gouged a chunk out of the sand nearby, a second hit the rock and whined off into space. Now they knew the location they were spreading out. Chagro's sixgun, better for infighting, cleared the leather without sound, a moving shadow jerked to the sixgun's blast and went down. The smell of powder was rank and strong; Chagro warmed to his task.

"Come on you lousy sons-of—" and he remembered the woman. He thumbed back his hat even as a rifle sounded from above—from the lava top it sounded like, but he didn't turn. They would be

50

closing in from all sides now—how many were there? He'd seen four but that didn't mean anything. A bulk took shape to his right and the '44 roared again. The Indian wheeled and collapsed, but not before he squeezed off a shot. The bullet tugged at Chagro's sleeve and he felt warm blood seep down his arm.

A horse screamed, there was the thud of hooves, then silence. The rifle up above was still, but a reddish glow began to touch sand and rock, fitful, then swiftly rising. Chagro jerked around to see flame leaping upon the lava top, a column of smoke and flame billowing upward into a dark sky.

"What—what is it?"

"Who cares? It's distraction. Let's get the hell out of here—they could be back after their dead."

He found the pony by feeling, by instinct; leaving the saddle, he transferred the food pack and canteen from the dead black and mounted, pulling the woman up behind him. They'd ride double for a quick getaway and after that, walk.

# FIVE

A half mile away Chagro swung to look. The column of flames had lessened, it was dying down so now only a ruby glow remained. There was no pursuit and they were in the clear, for the moment at least.

With time to think, he couldn't come up with a single answer. It was being borne in him that there was some mysterious personage meddling in his affairs, or trying to.

Who was it? The rider who'd picked up his track and followed after leaving the coach road? And he could have sworn somebody hailed him as he left the barranca. Not yelled, *hailed.* Was this the man, young, Annabelle said, who trailed but did not overtake her? And the fire on the lava crag—for a purpose, or horseplay? Damned funny sense of humor if it was humor. If not, who would have his, Chagro's, interest that much at heart?

Annabelle ground her knuckles into his back. "Are we going to stop soon?"

"We just started. Close your eyes. You can rest if you think you can."

Moonlight was a pale suggestion but sufficient glow to allow the horse to avoid rocks and clumps of bush. Here were occasional cacti, each plant outlined in silver halo, the spiny ocotillo all in bloom with its dark red flowers clear black against the branches, ironwood and thickets of scrub oak.

All this country now was familiar to him and he was free in it. Owned it. And despite the posse, the threat of Indians, and the throbbing of the flesh wound in his arm, he threw back his head and pulled the cool, bracing air deep into his lungs, and rejoiced in it. It smelled of the sun, the beat of the earth, of growing things. The desert was a friend, something first seen, then known, and loved ever after.

At midnight they threw off for short rest, Annabelle Weems sinking immediately to the ground. She gnawed a bit of jerky and drank from the canteen. Her face was uplifted to him, a vague blur in the darkness.

"Come down here," she said.

"No, we're going on. Get on your feet, let's move."

"*Now?*" she protested. "We've only been a few minutes! You call this a rest?"

Chagro's hands had been exploring the pony, withers, barrel, chest, the neck on both sides. He seemed fresh enough, nevertheless, from here on he'd carry the woman only. The horse flinched when Chagro touched a shoulder, bullet burned and faintly sticky.

"Knock it, will you?" Chagro growled to the woman. "You had some idea when you rode out after me. But I'm through arguing. It's go or stay, up to you."

She flared, "You don't show any mercy, do you? Look at me—I'm ready to drop!" For an answer Chagro picked up the reins; she leaped angrily to her feet and followed.

"You're a beast!"

"I've been called worse."

"I ache all over," she presently complained. Then, "I'm his wife but we never lived together."

"Now," he drawled, "how'd you manage that?" and added, "I like my women honest. Rough sometimes, but honest, if I have to take one to get the other. You're not coming across very good. Anyhow, what's it to me? Bellyache any more and I'll dump you right here. Your husband'll be along pretty soon—I've got a hunch he's hot on our tails right now."

"By God, I bet you would," she panted, "leave me here, I mean. I wouldn't put it past you one inch!"

The pony stumbled and Chagro halted at once. "Walk," he invited.

"What?"

"Get down. The luxury's over."

"How far?" she managed.

"Five miles. And don't think I'll carry you. Drop out and you stay."

He felt mean about it but if he didn't spur her on, they wouldn't get anywhere. She had to grow a few calluses in order to survive. Sure she was a woman but women weren't weaklings, needn't be. Well, hell. It wasn't his problem if Weems couldn't keep his wife. But he didn't know what to do if she wasn't able to take it. What if the redskins showed up?

Thirty-seven miles behind Chagro and the woman, Daniel Akins rode, Dan Akins in his calm and methodical way, turning a thing over in his mind and coming to a decision. He had put together the series of events since the start of this journey until it formed part of a pattern, the remainder of which was yet to be added. But he was pretty sure he knew what the answer would be. He also knew that when the chips were down, he would do what had to be done, no matter how much he hated it, but he would do it in his own fashion. Unless there was a way out.

It was the way out that concerned him. Ordinarily it helped to know the one you trailed, but Chagro Brannigan was in no way ordinary. He could act on impulse instead of reason, on instinct instead of method, true to no design and never to be predicted. The man who tried it was a fool, and somebody would die, maybe a lot of them. And Akins didn't want that if he could help it. Chagro, Akins thought, would make it to Mexico laughing in all their faces.

Which didn't bother Akins one bit, but it did bother Weems.

And Freeman? Freeman had all the earmarks of a gunslick, and in Akins's judgment, the kind to weasel when confronted, then blast the minute a man's back was turned. Weems, bitter, determined, would have his pound of flesh; Freeman, cold and deliberate, would have a cut of the reward.

Several times Akins had caught Weems's eyes on the dour one, speculation in that glance. It meant something, but Akins didn't know what. Weems had a notion in his head and sooner or later it would come out.

Akins knew well enough what Weems was thinking when the latter suddenly said, "S'pose Brannigan doubles back?"

Freeman turned his cold-fish stare. "Doubles back? What for? Of course, he won't. He'd be out of his head to."

Weems didn't answer, but it was plain his fear again curdled him. He looked at Freeman almost in despair. Shortly he pushed his horse up beside Freeman and blurted, "I want to talk to you."

"Well, talk."

"No, not here." Weems's head moved, indicating Akins. "Later. In private. I been watchin' you an' I think you're the man for me. I got a idea—"

"Later."

Talk ceased. Saddles creaked, the smell of horse sweat rising rank and sulfurous. Akins, who rode behind, digested what he'd heard and said nothing.

That night the two went into a huddle, and shortly Weems came to Akins and said, "You know I'm a man of property. I got my businesses, my investments, an' I'm wonderin' how they're gettin' on. My notion's they should be 'tended to.

Who's to do it if I don't? I been thinkin'—"

"Why don't you come out and say what you - mean? You want to go back."

Weems spat, testily. "No need to be so damn blunt! But yeah—guess that's about it. Still, you got the say-so an' if you lay your power on me, I got to go. I know I got a stake in this same's every other citizen in Dos Brazos, but bein' a man of business, it's natural I worry how things are goin'."

The situation was beginning to clear. Akins gave the speaker a cool, laconic inspection, then jerked a thumb at Freeman. "What about him?"

Weems had the grace to look flustered and he didn't meet Akins's eyes.

"Figuring to dig out, run on ahead, paid by you," Akins added. "That it? Why take a cut when you can get the whole thing?"

"Free country," Weems blustered. "Used to be a bounty hunter, he just told me. He'll do the job in my place. Mean you don't want him to flush Brannigan out? Mabbe I'll believe what I'm hearin', that Brannigan's a friend of yours an' you'd rather not have anybody flush 'im out, so's you can get there first and warn him."

Akins's face had seemed to settle. "I take exception to that," he said, quieter and quieter. He had also been standing loose and easy, now he moved back a step.

Freeman stiffened, Weems's face blanched. To Freeman, the deputy was an unknown quantity and therefore not to be braced. He didn't make a move, his hands well away from his guns. "No offense," Weems offered hurriedly. "I run off at the mouth sometimes, but I got a lot to worry me right now."

"That you have," Akins murmured, again pleasant. Freeman had relaxed, he was pasting on a narrow grin but it was stalemate and Akins knew it. Weems was like Sheriff Dawson in one respect; his feet wouldn't let his head get hurt, and no power in the world would keep the bounty hunter here if he didn't want to stay. It was big, empty country and if Freeman couldn't leave openly, he'd sneak away between dark and daylight. Orders from the acting law wouldn't hold him, and one of Akins's ironclad rules, adopted long ago, was never make a threat he couldn't back up. There was one way to stop Freeman and that was to kill him. Akins mulled the matter over, then nodded. "All right. S'pose you'll be pullin' out right away."

"The sooner, the better," Weems agreed, obviously relieved.

So the two would go. Tono didn't enter the picture at all, Tono was a different breed of cat. But besides a wife of only a few weeks, Weems owned a stage stop, the feed store, and a couple of bridges he'd flung across tributaries of the Little Caballa and on which he collected tolls. But what prodded Weems most was Annabelle. She'd had her eye out for any man who'd look at her and after Chagro came along, Chagro in particular. But being the independent sort, Chagro Brannigan wouldn't stand still for rope and halter or much of anything else unless he took a notion.

Akins sought out Tono who was sitting beside the fire. "You interested in going on? I'm givin' you a choice. This end of the posse's falling to pieces anyhow. The reward still stands but don't feel you're tied."

The Indian laid a handful of small twigs on the blaze, the twigs of the sort that wouldn't make any smoke. His saturnine face bent to the fire. "I got no wife." He glanced over his shoulder at Freeman and Weems, who had walked a bit apart. "No money either." He shrugged. "Money no mean anything to me. I no like trap. To him—" his head jerked, "money much important. Maybe sometime I like see this Chagro. One hell of a man, good for make tracks, tracks no lead nowhere. Long way to go for just see, though. What you say?"

Weems and Freeman seemed to be arguing about something. Weems gestured, shrugged in submission, and spread his hands. He looked over at the two beside the fire and lowered his voice.

Akins tipped coffee from the pot and sat back on his heels. "They're pullin' out," he said.

"I think you do all right 'lone anyhow, huh?" the Indian observed.

"We'll see. Never lay odds on a frog until he hops."

Weems left immediately, Freeman shortly after, as Akins expected. Sometime during the dark hours, Tono also drifted away. One of the three left because he couldn't trust his wife, a second drawn by the scent of blood, and the Indian, Tono, gone because he understood.

Akins faced the desert alone and for the first time

was glad of the badge. It carried weight and authority and because of it, men would listen. Maybe Chagro would listen. Give it all you have and trust to luck you get there in time, before Freeman. If not, trust the flamboyant Irishman not to do anything rash, because sure as hell, blood was going to be spread somewhere.

There was still the remainder of the posse that Akins was scheduled to meet in Matagordo but no assurance now that he would. For the first time, Akins allowed himself to speculate upon the possibility that they might already have laid hands upon both the missing thirty thousand and the three fugitives, and he knew what a stupid notion that was. He didn't know about the others, but whatever else Chagro might be, he was no fool.

A tiny blaze deep in the shelter of a rock fall was the second night's camp. Akins now hunkered alone beside the fire and ate his rations and considered the morrow. A straight line was the shortest distance between two points and still barring Indians, he was making better time alone.

Raised on the prairies, Akins had served in his earlier years as a scout for wagon trains traveling between Kansas and California and later, before his marriage, as a courier and in undercover work for the Army. He now felt a sense of returning to the trade he knew best, however brief that might be.

Carrie was a practical woman, she'd make out. He'd said that but winced to remember how Billy had begged to come along with him. Six was an impressionable age, he ran around shouting

*Bang!* with every stick he found. Maybe by the time the boy grew up, the country would be a better place to live in, farms and homes and settled government, the admiring awe for gunfighters and gunfighting worn out. A boy's father could hope so.

Ground currents of cooler air disturbed the blaze and from a far ridge, a coyote cried to the scattered stars. Akins lifted his head, listening, then rose quickly, coming up with his rifle in hand. He melted back into the deeper shadows, reached a fork in the rock fall, and here stationed himself. A horse somewhere off in the brush presently whinnied and his own horse, cropping grass in a small meadow nearby, sang out immediate answer.

"Halloo, there. Anybody home?" It was a white man, not an Indian, but a young voice with youth's squeakiness not quite gone out of it. Without lowering his rifle, Akins swung his head so the rock walls would echo the words to make their origin uncertain.

"Come on in."

"I'm alone, mister, and I got my hands up." Saddle leather creaked, and the newcomer stepped into the faint light of the fire, both arms upraised. Akins stared. It was only a big cheerful kid not dry behind the ears yet. Dressed in a buckskin coat, battered hat, and pants stuffed into dusty boots, with the biggest feet Akins had seen in all his life.

Akins stepped forward, still warily. "Sing out, boy. What's your name and where you bound?"

"Sean O'Donegal. Just passing through. My

horse must of smelled your horse an' sent the signal. I figured I better show myself." He grinned, a wide, friendly, unabashed grin and slowly lowered his hands. Huge, he was, even more so close up, with shoulders like an ox and a big, round kid face, and a fringe of reddish hair curled down over his collar in back. He wore two guns, one with the butt forward and the other turned backward and carried a long-barreled rifle in a shoulder sling. He folded to his heels and looked around curiously, as a youngster might do. Seeing Akins staring at the rifle, he promptly passed it over, stock first.

"Dan Akins' my name," the latter said. "You already seen the badge an' figured out the rest. Unusual piece of artillery you got here. What make is it? Never saw one like it before."

This Sean O'Donegal grinned again, a disarming, infectious grin. A little on the crocky side? Akins wondered. With all those guns, he was a walking arsenal, dangerous to have around unless it was all brag. A lot of kids did that, made them feel important. The next minute he changed his mind about one thing, at least.

"You like it? Made it myself. I ain't very bright, but some things I know to do and guns is one of 'em."

"Long barrel, more accuracy."

"Sure."

Akins played a sudden hunch. "You ride in from the east, from Dos Brazos way? Maybe you know the barrancas."

The youth shrugged his big shoulders. "Barranca—that mean rock? I seen some rocks, but then I seen a lot of rocks."

Akins handed the rifle back, barrel first, and the kid didn't flinch.

"There's Indians in these parts, you know. Or did you see any?" Belatedly Akins reached for the coffee pot with its still warm liquid, rinsed out a cup, filled and passed it over.

"Yeah. Plenty of Injun sign. Naked pony tracks, that'd only be Injuns, wouldn't it?" He indicated the star on Akins's chest, showing all his teeth eagerly as he did so. "Sure like to travel with you, mister, but guess you wouldn't want a kid tagging along. Ma says I got a jaw hinged on both ends."

"Where you from, originally?"

The kid finished the last of the coffee and handed the cup back. His interest seemed to have wandered, he looked back at Akins in apology. "Me? From Abilene. My Ma was there but she's not any more. Went East, I think she said." The young giant frowned. "Yeah, it was East."

"Don't you *know?*"

"Well, she didn't exactly say. Not right out, anyhow. Figure she'd had enough of me and didn't want me followin' her in case I had the notion. I grew up in a forest of legs."

"What?"

"I mean lookin' through 'em. In the saloon, see? She worked in the Dodge House and I just run around. Entertained myself till I learned how to talk to animals. You should hear me talk to a chicken! Answer back, too. Ma said I was half bushy and the other half just plain damned fool.

Don't kill squirrels either, only when I'm hungry. Then I guess I can eat about anything. I got a big appetite.'' Regretfully he got to his feet, and Akins, following him from those feet up, revised his earlier judgement. Six foot six, if he was an inch and the rest to match, and it occurred to Akins to wonder what the hell kind of horse this big lunk rode. Only about sixteen, Akins thought, and still growing. Hesitantly the boy indicated the badge. "If I could be of some help to you, I'd sure like to—"

"No. Afraid not."

"Yeah. I thought. Well, thanks for the coffee, Mr. Akins. I guess I'll be going."

"Where?" asked Akins, feeling oddly defeated. Somehow he liked the kid, wasn't sure about him, but liked him.

The boy shrugged. "California, I guess. I always wanted to see California. Heard a lot about it but never seen it. You been real nice. Maybe I'll see you again sometime."

"Not likely. I'm heading for Mexico, got business there."

"Oh. Mexico. Sure I can't tag along? No, s'pose not." The kid sighed. "I figured once I'd be a lawman, but the business would have killed me. No stomach for it. I never step on a bug, leastways, not when I know it. Birds are my friends. They can say a lot of things, birds can, if you let 'em."

"Wait a minute," Akins said gruffly. "You hungry?"

"Nah. I got that squirrel. Sure sorry to do it but I conked 'im with a rock."

"Rock? Why not a gun, the way you're braced?" Akins gestured. "Or they just for decoration?"

Sean O'Donegal sighed. "Figured the Injuns would hear. They were pretty close. Sure hated to eat my friend raw and that's what I done, Mr. Akins—ate him raw. See, I talk too much. I told you. G'night."

He faded into the darkness, silently despite his bulk. Akins sat motionless for some time until he heard the drum of retreating hooves. Out of the night, into the night again, a stray come and gone like an apparition. A forest of legs. Good God. Well, that was the way a kid would see it. What he said made sense, in his way. He had the simple literalness of a ten-year-old, but was he as bushy as he seemed? A big happy-go-lucky Mick, Irish as Paddy's pig with a name like that—if it was his name. He reminded Akins of somebody he had seen or known, but the who escaped him.

He didn't drop down from heaven, he must have come from somewhere. Akins realized he hadn't actually said. If from the east, he would have crossed Weems, back pedaling for Dos Brazos. Akins suddenly remembered the boy hadn't said much of anything else to tie to, either. A name that might or might not be his own, a destination, maybe. He just might have dropped in to look the situation over, Akins decided. But what for? Akins began to feel uneasy without knowing why, like clouds gathered in the offing. Maybe he should have let the kid stay, to keep him out of trouble. Only he didn't look like the trouble sort.

Akins grunted, killed the remnants of the fire,

then picked up his gear, and choosing a spot some distance from the first one, made fresh camp. He sat for some time, listening keenly to the night and hearing nothing; all was peaceful and still. Akins got the horse, moved the animal to a different place, secured him, then curled up in the sand for a few hours' sleep. There were a lot of fellows, Akins told himself, roaming around the country, young ones as restless as he was himself at that age, seeking excitement and change—was that so unusual? Yet he couldn't rid himself of the feeling of familiarity. A turn of head, the lift of a sentence—it still eluded him.

# SIX

Avoiding the larger and more populated El Paso, Chagro pushed on to Isleta. Isleta was a single dusty street meandering through a huddle of adobe buildings, a public square, and a tumbledown church. This was all of the place. A mud settlement dignified only by a name, it nevertheless played host to traffic of many levels. Situated with the front open to the United States and the rear virtually in Mexico, to fugitives it was a last hop before fading across the border to anonymity.

Chagro had a reason for the stop and the reason was Annabelle Weems. He had many friends in Isleta, as he had friends everywhere who would cover for him, lie, and even provide shelter for indefinite periods, if the occasion demanded.

Luck was with him. Grapevine had it that a party of emigrants accompanied by military escort was to pass through Isleta heading north the next morning, and Chagro, safely ensconced in a back room of Nora's cantina—a room he'd used before, sent an emissary to verify.

It was true. Word, he judged, would not yet have reached the village of his wanted status, so he went boldly to make the arrangements himself, thereby getting the jump on Annabelle, who would be all too eager to broadcast the news once she found out what he was up to.

This devious bit of business, however, left Annabelle to sputter angrily over the announcement of her impending departure. The message was delivered not in person by Chagro—he didn't even have the decency, she raged, after last night—but by a Mexican urchin who ducked in and dived out before she could question him.

Chagro was free, at least as free as possible under the circumstances, and he congratulated himself on a job well done. A load had rolled off his shoulders, a relief that ordinarily would have occasioned a good, roaring drunk. But discretion being the better wisdom of valor, he greeted old friends, had a few drinks with them, then got down to private affairs.

He traded the pony to a Maricopa for a rangy, sorrel gelding and a few dollars to boot. Then he bought a Mexican saddle, a canteen, and pack. After this, he stabled the beast in the shed behind the cantina, consumed quantities of chili and tortillas washed down with fiery tequila, and rolled in for what was left of the night.

Shortly after dawn, Jose, the Mexican youngster, touched his arm. "*Senor*, wake up. I have *sometheeng* to tell you. *Mamacita* say wake up

68

thees Chagro—hurry! Thees man, he ask about you, see?"

Chagro sat up yawning and ran a hand through his tousled hair. He spoke Spanish like a native and what ensued was in Spanish. The man was thin, stoop shouldered, and his hair was black. He had a scar on his right cheek. Did *Senor* Chagro know such a man? The initials on the holster were D.F.; he, Jose, had gotten close enough to see, also to open the man's pack. The pack had *nada* in it though, which was very disappointing. What did he want *Senor* Brannigan for?

"Not for any good," Chagro grunted, because he had a hunch. Thin, stoop shouldered, with a scar. Could that be Freeman? Tricky with a gun, from Dos Brazos. Chagro had seen him hanging around town and it was that place of origin that pricked up Chagro's ears the most. Dos Brazos, Freeman, the posse. Was Dawson here too and the rest of the bunch? That was fast work. He questioned the boy but the lad shook his head. He knew nothing about a fat one with a star on his chest, nor anybody else strange. Only one asked and *Mama-cita* had warned him to answer nothing. As if he would have done so anyway!

Chagro fished a coin from his pocket and held it out.

The boy drew back. *"Senor,"* he said with injured dignity, "of thees you have no need!"

Chagro grinned. "So? Well, take it for the next time, then. And keep out of strange packs—see?" He ruffled the boy's hair and watched him scamper off.

Presently the door opened and Nora came in bearing a tray, on it fresh tortillas, eggs and a slab of ham, and coffee steaming in a huge mug. She set the tray down.

"Thees one who ask for you—you know heem?"

"I know him. Man by the name of Freeman. Gunslinger from Dos Brazos, I'd bank on it."

"Then you stay here," Nora decided positively. "*Comprende?* Nobody fin' you here. You on the run, hey? Thees place is safe."

"You're a good sport, Nora," Chagro approved, "and I appreciate the offer, but I'll be pullin' out. That he-coyote's an omen. By this time, it's dead or alive for me and I don't want to clutter up your place with the dead an' dyin'!"

Nora was big, pillowlike, and shrewd in judgement of the many who passed through her place. She regarded Chagro with her head tipped to one side and eyes narrowed. "You make joke," she accused. "Always make joke. You be careful not make to wrong people, eh?" It was the measure of *Mamacita* that she didn't ask what the trouble was all about. It was enough that she and her whole *familia*—grandmother and four *ninos*, twins of four years, a daughter of twelve, and her next eldest, Jose—would ask no questions. Sufficient that Chagro was here and that he needed help. He should go out the back way if he must leave, she said. This man was even now in the dining room waiting for his order of breakfast, which would be delayed as long as possible. There would be a pack of food tied on Chagro's *caballo*, his horse, which would be fed and watered. Jose would do that. Jose would hurry and the horse would be ready.

She pointed to the tray. "Eat, then," she ordered.

"Takes *pesos* to buy beans," Chagro growled. "This time I'm payin', see?"

Her heavy brows shot up. "Go to hell," she advised crisply and waddled out, slamming the door.

Ten thousand in the bucket; well, he'd come back and do something for them all, so help him God, he would. If he came out of this alive, he would.

But Chagro was curious. He wanted a look anyway, to make sure it was Freeman. There was a kitchen and from the kitchen issued delicious smells. From the kitchen also, eventually, would issue the stranger's breakfast. Chagro winked at Elmira and chucked her under the chin. "Some day I'm comin' back and carry you off," he said, sidestepped *Mamacita* and a table loaded with chili-in-the-making, and stationed himself where he could see yet not be seen.

One look at that glowering countenance told Chagro what he wanted to know. It was Freeman, all right.

"Keep him here as long as you can," he suggested to *Mamacita* and stepped out the back door, whistling.

She moved after him swiftly despite her bulk. "Better you hurry, huh? *Vamos!* Thees man mean beeg trouble—I can tell." She glanced over her shoulder, then back at Chagro anxiously. "Eef he is hunting you, why you not go—the stable ees

71

that way, *el caballo* ready. What you going to do, anyhow?"

"Have me a good drink, I owe myself that much. A farewell drink for the long, hot trail. So long, *Mamacita.*" He was gone with a swing of his shoulders, she stared after him. Crazy fool in *Norteamericano* came to her mind and she shook her head. He bore no charmed life. One of these days—

It was too early for regular customers, but there was one man in the saloon, seated alone at a table with his back to the door. A bottle and glass stood before him but he was not drinking.

"I'll be—" Chagro muttered and entered quietly. He advanced and laid a hand on Dan Akins's shoulder. "How, boy?" Akins swung, started to rise but the hand pushed him back. Chagro slipped into the chair opposite, grinning broadly.

"A star, I see. You, the law? Now how'd that happen? You old ridgerunner, you! Damn, I'm glad to lay eyes on you again—it's been a long time. Too long!"

Akins got his wits back, he took a deep breath; what he felt was shame. "You know what I'm here for," he said. "I'm authorized to take you in."

"Yeah, sure. Don't make any false moves!" as Akins's hand shifted on the tabletop. "I got a '44 aimed straight in your gut. Now you wouldn't want me to do anything unfriendly, would you?"

Akins sighed and his shoulders relaxed. "You damn fool," he murmured. "Haven't you got sense enough not to show yourself in public? Freeman's here already, gunnin' for you."

72

"I know that," Chagro said cheerfully. "Left him over at Nora's boltin' down the chow. A reward out for me?"

"A thousand," admitted Akins, "fifteen hundred for all three." He looked at the man before him, looked him over thoroughly and saw no change. Still the same broad and open smile, the shock of sandy hair, the powerful shoulders. A fine figure of a man, a hero in the boy's eyes. An outlaw. "Billy's fine," Akins said abruptly.

"Still shootin' his guns? All kids have the bug. He'll get over it. Carrie?"

"Fine." Damned if Carrie wouldn't send her best regards if she knew Chagro was here. "The boy's scared to death of rattlers though, since that time. Just as well."

Chagro gestured to the badge. "You sure didn't waste much time gettin' here. And where's the switch? Thought Dawson had it."

Akins told him that Dawson couldn't hack it. Gone home sick, and Franks left.

Chagro's brows raised. "Where's the rest of 'em? You mean I don't rate more action than that? My popularity must be slippin'." The big man lifted a hand to the bartender, who had been waiting for the greeting. "How's she goin', Pablo?"

The bartender ducked his head and showed all his teeth happily.

"*Bueno, Senor* Chagro, *bueno*. Two since you come see us last—eight *muchachos* I got now."

"Eight! I'll be damned. You're a good man, Pablo, don't let anybody tell you different. How about rustlin' up an extra glass? Never did fancy a man drinkin' alone."

"Oh, *si!* Quickly!"

Pablo set it before him, Chagro shoved it over and Akins filled it, then his own. Akins took a swallow of his whiskey. "Oughtn't to be tellin' you this," Akins grumbled, "but what else? There was six. All gone home except Freeman. Weems hired 'im."

"Sure, sure," breathed Chagro. "That'd be Weems, all right. Scared for his bridges and his stores. I had his wife on my neck for awhile."

"Uh-huh." Akins nodded. "I wondered. Planned on asking you about that. Indian pony tracks, then a big heavy brute led me to the lava, and after that the pony again. You had some kind of a scrap there. Indians jump you?" Chagro nodded. "Then I saw a woman's footprints all over the place. Wait'll Jeff finds out she's gone."

"Gone all right but headed back," Chagro explained, adding, "Damndest uproar I ever had on any trail, bar none. Bitch, bitch, bitch—man couldn't keep his mind on his business. He can have her back with my blessin'. I hate to say it but they deserve each other."

Akins's lips quirked. He looked Chagro over again and said at last, "Let me take you in. It'll save a lot of trouble and I'll get you back safe, you got my word on it. You know where the money is. Turn it over, release yourself to my custody an' I'll do everything I can to get you off."

"Not a chance." Chagro grinned broadly. "I might make a suggestion of my own. Throw in with me an' we'll hit the high spots—only I know

74

you wouldn't. You got Carrie and the kid. I got two men dead behind me and the thirty thousand. You believe they're goin' to stand still for that?"

"I think I can figure out what happened," Akins said. "You're not one to shoot men down in cold blood. That'd be somebody with a murderin' brand on him and that ain't you."

"I'm to blame, and nothing you say or do will make any difference. No, you'll go decent in bed when your time comes but it's not in the cards for me."

"You talk wild!" Akins said sharply. "Ought to get married, settle down, and have some kids yourself. Find out what it's all about. I'm new at this kind of law game, but I think I know how it's done. But damn it, my feelings tell me otherwise! Look, man. Stop and think. Sure you know where it'll end if you keep on. The time to get out from under is now. I can't see you goin' on like this. I'll do all in my power to—"

"No good. I hear what you're sayin' and you're not sayin' it to me. Dan, you're a good boy an' you'll do fine. I wish things were different—sometimes I think that, but they won't be. It's too late. You know it as well as I do."

They sat silent, two men who liked each other, with the liking apparent. Two who would have trusted each other with their lives but who were a world apart. "Where's the others in it with you?" Akins hadn't expected Chagro to answer; the latter shook his head.

"Where I ought to be right now," he said. "That joker will be finishin' his breakfast pretty soon and

I got to be on my way. Something you forgot to tell me. Dawson must of split the posse—where's the rest of 'em?"

Akins sighed. "You keep yours an' I'll keep mine," he said. "Another drink?"

"Nope. You don't tie my feet that way."

"Then skin out of here right now, for God's sake," Akins said tightly, "before I do something I'll be sorry for, or take a crack at it."

"You won't," said Chagro gently. "I step out that door and I'm on Mexican soil. You know what that means. You could have gone through the motions an' arrested me but I'd never go back—I don't fancy my neck bein' stretched with a rope. If I went with you, I'd have no chance, no chance at all. And what makes you think you'd get me back? Even if you tried, they'd kill you to get to me and where would that leave Carrie and the kid? I'm money in the pot. My path's laid out already—a straight one; aim high an' fall hard. Freeman's after me, all of Dos Brazos' after me, the rest of Dawson's posse. That's about six of 'em, I figure. Afraid it's no go, not your way."

Akins shook it all together, boiled it down, and said quietly, "There'll be another time."

"Yeah. But I won't shoot you an' you won't shoot me."

"Don't count on it," said Akins with weary stubbornness. "If it's me against you, it'll be the end of one of us. I hope to God it don't come to that. If I'm still alive, I wouldn't want it on my conscience, but that's the way it's got to be."

"At least you stated it plain," Chagro growled.

"I'll try to keep out of your way."

"Be careful of Freeman," Akins said. "Freeman's a killer, it's written all over him. We've both seen his kind before. A bounty hunter with real blood in his eye. Anywhere below the border, he's just plain dangerous, above, he's got the law on his side. You haven't. You're going to go down one way or another, sure's God made little green grapes. I'll hate to see you dead."

"Happens to all of us," Chagro said cheerfully. "I been warned, and thanks. I'll remember that. Well, take care of yourself, son—an' keep those hands in plain sight, huh?"

Akins looked up, shaking his head. "Tell me one thing," he said. "Did you have a gun on me awhile ago?"

The Irishman's laugh rang out. "Hell no, you old mossback—hell, no." He backed easily, raised an arm in salute, slipped through the doorway, and was gone.

It wasn't until later Akins remembered he hadn't mentioned the boy—Sean O'Donegal. And now, recalling those mannerisms, the turn of head, he knew where the similarity lay. If Chagro Brannigan didn't know, he'd find out and if Akins's guess was correct, Chagro was in for a shock.

The deputy eyed the bottle before him and knew he wanted to get drunk. Stinkin', lousy, boozed-to-the-chops, rotten drunk.

He tipped the bottle. "I'm goin' to get drunk," he said.

Pablo looked over sympathetically." *Si, Senor.*

Me too. *Excepto* who would tend the bar?"

Akins considered the bottle before taking the plunge, then pushed it back. He had things to do, what the hell was he doing sitting here? At the moment, he was filled with self-disgust and felt like the man on the sawhorse—neither straddling the damn thing nor falling off. The star meant something, all right. If he had Dawson here, he'd tell him to shove it where it did most good. He'd never wanted the job in the first place but what could he do about it now? His course was laid out for him, too, and nothing to do but go on and trust to luck, or miracles.

Akins swore, clapped his hat on his head, and went out. On the porch he halted suddenly, swung and retraced his steps, laid a silver dollar on the bar, and again turned out. That glimpse had spotted Freeman emerging from the cantina, the gunman paused to pick his teeth and consider the street this early morning. The street was empty; Chagro had gone. Once more Akins whirled, beat it through the saloon, and stepped out the back door so recently vacated by Chagro. From a distance the faint drum of hooves reached him.

There was a rancho forty miles into Mexico where a canny fugitive, knowing the area, might stop for a fresh horse. It had been done before. And weren't there villages, Santa Lucas, Camargas, some fifty miles or so beyond that? And El Seco. Otherwise the hills were empty, save for bandits, Indians, and rattlesnakes. It was rugged country.

Freeman had entered the saloon, taking all the time in the world. Pretty sure of himself, was

Akins's thought, and wondered. The deputy got his horse and walking the animal, left the settlement by a circuitous route. He rode steadily for an hour, not seeking out Chagro's trail but playing his hunch, and at the end of the hour, he secreted the horse and himself in a thicket of paloverde and ironwood, to wait.

For all that, Akins's travel had garbled up the tracks and it took Freeman an appreciable time to show. And when he did, Akins stared in amazement. He had Annabelle Weems with him.

# SEVEN

Akins stepped out suddenly from the thicket, rifle up. "Hold it—right there!"

Freeman jerked the horse to its haunches in surprise, the other hand automatically streaking for his gun.

"Wouldn't do it!" Akins's rifle barked, neck creasing the animal, which went into a plunge, tipping the man off balance and near unseating him. Annabelle's sorrel jerked away, spooked by the commotion. "Next time I won't miss," Akins pointed out. "Keep your fist away from that '44. Now set still, both of you." He stared at Annabelle, disheveled, dusty, trail battered, and aggressive—the aggressiveness of a man, he realized.

"Where the hell did you come from?" Freeman snarled. "I thought I outran you."

"Have to get up earlier in the morning," Akins pointed out. "Kind of dumb, I'd say. I come out just ahead of you. You won't live long with that kind of carelessness, if you'd been of a mind to get away with anything. What's she doing with you?"

Freeman eased back in the saddle. "My passport to Brannigan."

"Didn't know you needed one."

Annabelle broke in. "He kidnapped me and brought me here! He made me come with him. I told him I wasn't in love with Mr. Brannigan but he wouldn't listen!"

Kidnapped? Her hands weren't tied, no marks of rope on her wrists. Slyness whipped across Annabelle's small pointed face, and something else, so swiftly come, swiftly gone that Akins couldn't define it. Spite? That was it. A woman scorned, he thought, ah, hell, and like Chagro, wished her the blackest luck definable—Jefferson Weems, her avenging husband.

Akins spat. "Looks to me like you come of your own free will," he observed. "Can't hold a man on that. You—Mrs. Weems, I got no truck with you, and no authority. But one thing I will say, you're not makin' it any easier on yourself. What's your husband going to do? Because he'll be along, you know. Figure I wouldn't want to be in your shoes when he catches up."

"I'm not afraid of him! I left him and that's that! I won't be tied like one of his prize horses. I'll show him!"

"Not fitting for a woman to go traipsing off across country this way," Akins pursued. "You got to think of Jefferson, too. You married him fair an' square. He's a rich man, you're a rich woman. Not every day a gal gets a nest like that. He'll tame. Right now he's scared of you, that's why he acts like he does. If he was sure of you, he'd relax. That way you could be happy together, but you got to give him a chance."

Annabelle's eyes had narrowed. "What you picking up the cudgel for him for? I thought you didn't like him."

"I don't, not like he is, but you makin' him that way. Man can take only so much, then he busts, one way or another. His come out in bad temper. You married a man, not a plaster saint. You got to think of that, too."

Annabelle shoved her twists of red hair back from her face, impatiently skewering it behind her ears. "Well, if you think I'm going crawling back, you've got another think coming. So you see, Mr. Deputy Akins, your little lecture has fallen on stony ground."

Akins said mildly, "Mind tellin' me what you do want?"

She and Freeman exchanged glances. "She wants you should mind your own damn business," Freeman snapped.

Akins stepped back and motioned with his rifle. "You can go on." He got to his own horse, watched them ride off. Did Freeman really believe Chagro was gone on the woman and would stand still for some kind of trap? Maybe it hadn't taken much talking; Freeman had his own plum in sight. And what was really the matter with her? Put all together, Akins could come up with his own theory; impulse had kicked her over the traces and plain mean bullheadedness kept her running. She'd gone too far to turn back. Akins spat again when his thoughts shifted to Freeman. That she sure had. Why had he bothered anyway? He'd gone a hell of a long way out on a limb painting Weems the sterling character he wasn't. Let 'em fight their own battles. They were in for plenty of them unless Weems was a real forgiving soul, and forgiving, Akins guessed, wasn't one of Jefferson Weems's strong points. In the meantime, she could be a lot of trouble.

Steady riding brought Akins to Bakeoven Pass, a hogback ridge cutting a tumbled, rocky area from east to west, this some fifteen miles from Isleta. There was no sign of Freeman and the woman. Here and yonder, pierced only by the upthrust arms of the giant cactus, was a stretch of desert that, if he were to follow this route and unless Freeman, unfamiliar with the country as he was, wasted time and effort going the long way, would bring him out ahead of the two travelers, to El Seco. If they chose Santa Lucas or Camargas, or if Chagro were in one of the latter two, he, Akins, had lost out.

Late that afternoon, he crossed tracks of Indians, and still later, those of a pair of shod horses he was certain belonged to Freeman and Annabelle Weems. He saw where they had stopped to rest, then gone on. Their trail pointed toward El Seco. Akins made his circle movement, by judicious maneuvering cut a mile off his journey and emerged that mile ahead of the two. It was near dusk when Akins made camp; the others, he judged, would be doing the same.

He rose at midnight, in pale moonlight and on a

rested horse, he pushed on toward the village. He was now a considerable distance ahead, and in cool gray dawn of morning, he reached the adobe squattle that was El Seco.

It was even smaller than he remembered. The deputy stabled his horse, took a half-hour rest himself, and as soon as the cafe's door opened, ate his first full meal in three days. Shortly he left, toured the town swiftly and methodically, then with the knowledge that Chagro Brannigan was not, nor had he been here, got his horse and put the village behind him.

As he left the settlement, taking a western exit, he kept to the rocky areas where tracking would be most difficult to follow. The trail presently swung north and east and he perceived in the far distance two riders. Akins faded into a heavy copse of cactus and ocotillo the better to see, then satisfied, traveled on. It was Freeman and the woman, still on course for El Seco. The deputy pulled his hat down against the rising glare of sun and headed into it.

Santa Lucas and Camargas. Akins's mind carefully turned over each of these, rummaging their possibilities from Chagro Brannigan's standpoint.

Santa Lucas lay southeast of Dry Woman Buttes, in an arid cup of surrounding hills—good shelter but not too easy to get in and out of. The ridge around it could harbor bandits, Indians, and the rocks themselves were an effective barrier to hasty departure, if the need arose. Santa Lucas was a very old, very small village; established by

Franciscan friars sometime in the mid-sixteen hundreds, it boasted a spring of excellent water but, Akins thought, that was all.

Camargas was fully as small but lay on a semi-sheltered plain more open to access, and to exit. Camargas was also old, also had good water, which was the reason for its existence. Camargas, then, Akins decided.

Matagordo was a full seventy miles east; Akins had considered it with long, long thoughts and discarded Matagordo. With no posse left at this end of the line, let the rest of it shift for itself. Basically, Akins could have said he still didn't know what to do; one thing he did know: that where the Irishman was, there was bound to be explosive action, and he wanted to be in on it. Hope had faded that he could induce Chagro to give himself up but there might be another way. If Chagro Brannigan was in Camargas—and Akins wanted to bet Chagro was—he'd have to come up with some plan to get the gold out. Until he did, until he made a move in that direction, Akins could do nothing.

With dusk, Chagro had entered Camargas. He had put up his horse and sought out the one saloon, slaking his travel thirst with mescal, a home-grown product here favored over tequila.

The cantina, small, narrow, dim, lighted only by flickering candles in sconces mounted on the walls, was nearly deserted. Only one large youth leaned elbows on the bar at its far end, and a couple of Mexicans sat at gaming tables desultorily playing; they did not look up as he entered.

There was no back-bar mirror; these small native places, skin poor, rarely boasted such luxury. However, Chagro felt the weight of scrutiny upon him.

He turned to study the young one briefly and dismissed the suspicion; it was nobody he knew. But someone who knew him? Chagro addressed himself to his drink, settled up, and left the place, stirred and uneasy without knowing why.

He paused in the dimness of the palm-thatched porch to roll and light a cigarette, taking his time at the chore, and it was here the Seminole found him. One moment Chagro was standing alone, the next the tall shadow loomed at his elbow, cat-silent as always.

"A good ride?"

Chagro let his breath out slowly, his hand fallen away from his hip. "A hot one. Dutch around?"

The Seminole, whose name nobody knew, spoke English very well and with only careful inflection. "He is here. In a cellar room of Madame Guise's rooming house, as we planned. We have been holing up there waiting for you. I am glad you have come. Sometimes I think that Dutch—no matter. He will look to you to lead, you can keep him on a tight rein. It is all over town that you are here, but the town will close around you, it will say nothing. Pilar was asking about you."

"Pilar. And Madame Guise?"

"At her same place at the end of the street. There was no trouble on your journey?"

"Not what you would call trouble." Chagro's

cigarette, flipped on a fingernail, struck the dust in a shower of sparks. "So far as I know, nobody tailed me, but Akins will be along sooner or later, and Freeman. Freeman's a hound dog on the scent and Akins wants to reform me. Been deputized."

"Freeman? The one from Dos Brazos? A gunman, I think."

"I'll take care of Freeman when the time comes. Know anybody in there?" Chagro jerked his head to the saloon entrance behind him.

"No. Once in awhile somebody passing through, mule trains and the like but not many of those; the trains, as you know, will start later. Not many otherwise find their way to this place."

"You'd know this one if you saw him," Chagro grunted. "About ten feet tall and all hunk. Seemed to be interested but maybe I'm only imaginin' things."

"Do you think he recognized you?"

"Don't think so. How could he? Never saw him before in my life."

The Indian said nothing further and they turned together into the dark, past the village well with its cluster of palms and on to the end of the street.

Madame Guise, who preferred to be called Mama Guise, claimed direct blood line with the Guise family of Europe—royalty of de Lorraine fame. Which could have been true, since many such splinters of ruling classes had broken away to invade the New World. Years ago she'd drifted from the old port of New Orleans where, in her heyday, she was the toast of the waterfront. She still spoke forcefully of returning to France and wresting hereditary titles and lands from the Bourbon-Orleans clan, but she would never depart her corner of Mexico. She loved it here. An old warhorse who made no bones about it, she clutched the whole world to her ample bosom. Ten yards of linsey-wolsey made her a dress, she boasted, and two chairs to plant it on, which was patently true.

It was a meeting impossible to bypass. Chagro was a favorite and she greeted him as a long, lost son. "My God, boy, you're a sight for sore eyes! Where you been keepin' yourself? Not married yet? Well, we'll have to see what we can do."

"I didn't bring you a damned thing. No gifts, nothing."

"Pah! Who wants gifts? You brought yourself. Come sit beside me—no, sit here."

Later, when he could get away, Chagro met the Seminole. "A lot of woman."

"A lot of woman," acknowledged the Indian, and neither meant disrespect. They let themselves down the dark stairs and into the large room lit by candlelight, the candles being stuck in necks of bottles, with other bottles and glasses at the ready. Here were tables and chairs, and at a table with no patience at all, Dutch Gault fidgeted.

"Thought you'd never get here." He sneered. "The huggin' an' kissin' all over?"

Chagro ignored that. He pulled up a chair and sat down, the Seminole did likewise, and business was discussed back and forth for a time. The canvas bag with the thirty thousand in it was hidden in a rock fall in a remote area southeast of town. Four miles, maybe five. Tricky to locate and get to, and safe as a church.

But Dutch Gault continued to be truculent, a truculence that challenged, which could be seen and felt. Socializing on any level was beyond his ken and he had no patience for it; waiting rankled him.

"I make a move we get right on with it," he began. "I got a plan—"

"No plan, yet. We're going to sit tight for awhile."

"Sit tight—what for? We wait till the wolves come nippin' at our heels? That what you say? I favor to get out of here while we can. Make a run for it. You say Akins is comin' on—"

"Akins can't do anything. We're in Mexico, remember? He can dog our heels till doomsday and unless we make a move back to the States, we're safe."

"An' the cash? What we goin' to do with that, sit on it till it hatches?" Gault's heavy face had settled in stubborn, bitter lines. He was a square and solid man, with a shock of night-black hair curled down over a sweating forehead and a pair of muddy eyes, which could change color with temper, and had changed now. He stared at Chagro, who seemed to stare it out. "You're runnin' this shebang," he managed at last, "an' if you say wait, I guess we got to wait. But I don't like it—I don't like it at all! With all that money—"

"All that money is just the trouble," murmured Chagro. "You want to put it on your back and pack it off—how long you think we'd last? Getting out's not going to be as easy as gettin' in. Nobody's going to do us any harm here. Pretty girls, plenty of mescal, a fiesta every night, if we want it. What's the hurry?"

Dutch's heavy lips pinched tight. "Then give me my share!" he burst out. "Divide it an' I'll be gone by mornin'. It's my right—I got a third of that damn money I sweat for comin' to me an' I aim to have it. It ain't goin' to cramp you none, an' you can do's you damn please with the rest. But I'm takin' my share now!" Dutch had half risen from his chair, hand whipped to his gun; Chagro was there before him. The Indian's own weapon was out and leveled; now he relaxed, dropping the '44 back in the holster.

"Sit down," Chagro invited smoothly and gestured. "Cool off. You're not going anywhere. I'll decide when it's to be divided. Sure, you'll get your share, you killed two men for it, but not yet. Want to blow the whole deal? We stand or fall together. That's the way we started out an' that's the way we finish—together. Seminole, you ain't said a word. What you think?"

"I think there is somebody wants to see you," the Indian said in his soft voice and gestured to the door.

The girl Pilar stood there, she flung herself ecstatically upon Chagro, who rose to sweep her off her feet and swing her about in a mighty hug.

"How long you have been gone!" Her face, perfectly oval, flushed under the soft brown; her eyes were big and hot and black and shone only for him. "It has been a long time!"

"Too long. Hey—save some for later!" He disengaged her arms and stood back to survey her. "Prettier than ever, pretty as a picture with those black curls an' red ribbon." His eyes slid over her narrowly. "Maybe a mite fatter, though," and ducked her upflung arm.

"You say you come back and marry me. *Bueno*—when is the wedding, eh?" She twirled before him, all vibrant life in her flounced multi-colored skirts. The skin of her throat and breast, the latter half bared by the low ruffled blouse, had a luster all its own. "Or—you got another woman? If you got another woman, I kill her—I tear her to pieces!"

"No other woman." Chagro laughed, then had an uneasy memory. By now, Annabelle, the red haired, temper-raddled Annabelle, was miles away and still going.

Sunk into his chair, Gault watched Chagro with an inscrutable, heavy-lidded glance and the Seminole watched Gault. To the dark-browed Gault, the Irishman's happy-go-lucky temperament and zest for living were enigmas and therefore to be distrusted; in his mind, the need for the company of women was a weakness and because Chagro Brannigan weakened to it, his supremacy was to be questioned. Brute force was the only rule Gault knew. Women were merely a means to an end, to be used summarily when needed. He looked at Pilar and Pilar looked back at him.

The girl said for Chagro's ears alone, "That one—Gault. There is murder in his head. Shoot him now or he will give much trouble later. Hear me! I speak truth."

Chagro laughed, gave a pat to her backside and sent her from the room. "I'll be along in a few minutes."

"Where?" she pouted.

"By God," he roared, "right here and now if you don't get going!"

She vanished with a flip of her bright skirts, the door swung shut behind her. Chagro lifted out his gun and laid it on the table.

"There it is. Is this a partnership, share an' share alike? War or peace? If we're goin' to have trouble, let's have it right now. Dutch, you want to start? Seems you got something in your head I had no hand in putting there."

Dutch stared at the gun, then slowly spread his hands, signifying retreat. "All right," he growled. "You got it. Pick up your gun, I won't give no trouble." He put on a grin. "Wouldn't cut down on a friend, would you? I git itchy thinkin' about all that money, that's all."

There was no use bucking the big man now, Gault thought. He had it all in the hollow of his hand. But there would be another time, a better day, and then he'd take all of it, not part. All. The Indian first, the watchful Indian. Then the big man. There would be a way.

Gault smiled again. "You win," he repeated.

The Seminole did not smile. The two rose and they all filed out.

# EIGHT

At noontime, Chagro went to check his horse. After three straight nights of excesses, he'd slept late—luxuries so seldom enjoyed he'd endeavored to make up for lost time. He had eaten a leisurely breakfast, then as had become his custom, strolled down to the livery stable in the heat of the day.

There was a watering trough and a corral with a fence, and behind him was a figure leaning on the bars. Chagro ignored it and walked on by, whistling the tune *Garry Owen* between his teeth.

"There's a man watching you from behind the cantina," that figure said.

"Yeah. I know." Chagro whirled about and came face to face with his mentor. "Who are you, anyway? Saw you staring at me in the saloon the other night—who sent you to dog my trail?"

"Nobody." The kid backed up a step. "Nobody sent me. I'm on my own—honest! I just wanted to see you, see what you looked like close up. That's all. Guess I been botherin' you some. I'm sure sorry. Never meant to—"

"Oh, for Christ's sake, stop babbling! So you wanted to see me." Chagro bit down on his temper and added more mildly, "Might I ask why?"

"Well," the kid faltered, "I guess I know you even if you don't know me. Maybe you better look at me, real close."

Chagro took the youth apart, piece by piece, and shook his head. "What's your name?—if you got one."

"I talked to Mr. Akins—Deputy Akins. He knows who I am, I think he does, anyway. It was me who went back and forth to cover your tracks. Then I hid up in the barranca an'—"

"*What?*"

The youngster gulped. "Yeah. I shot at 'em, the canteens I mean, so's they wouldn't get started after you so soon. I killed one of the horses though, by mistake—sure sorry about that. Wouldn't of done it 'cept I was in such a big hurry."

"Look," Chagro said, "I don't understand this at all. An' I'm gettin' pretty damned out of patience an' when I'm out of patience, I'm apt to take somethin' apart. Who the hell are you, anyway?"

"I'm comin' to that, but I got to tell you. The rest of it, I mean. I figured you'd be mad, but not this mad. But I still got to tell you. See, it was me up on the lava, too. I made that fire. Guess you wondered about that. Then I watched over the woman, kinda, because I thought she was yours, an'—" The boy was sweating, nervous with his unburdening; he'd backed to the corral fence and

94

stood shoulders against it, his eyes not meeting Chagro's eyes.

Chagro's teeth clenched, his hands balled to fists. "I can see this has something to do with me, but damned if I know what. I ask you again—what's your name?"

"Same's yours," the kid blurted, "—Brannigan. Guess you're my Pa. Hello—Pa."

"Huh?" The earth dropped from beneath Chagro's feet, he stared stupidly. At that moment a rifle ball could have hit before him and he wouldn't have known it.

"Yeah," the boy said. "I said it was O'Donegal to Akins—I told him that. Figure I didn't want to go blabbin' it all around, not then anyway, leastways not until I told you first."

"That was—real thoughtful of you," Chagro heard himself say. "You—my kid?" Wildly he racked his brain. Which one? He'd left a string of—one was enough, he decided. One was enough, by God. Every man scattered himself around some. But not every time one rose in the flesh to confront you. Chagro's knees felt rubbery, all at once he wanted to sit down. "Let's walk," he said. The kid fell dutifully in behind. "Not there," Chagro ordered gruffly, "up here."

"All right—Dad."

Chagro's ears burned. He'd have to get used to it. Dad. Pa. Oh hell, he thought. He looked over at the kid and frowned. How'd he know it was his son? "What's the rest of it—your name, I mean."

"Sean."

"Real good Irish."

"Yeah. I mean, yes, sir."

"Your Ma's?"

"Belle." It was true all right, Chagro remembered that much. There was one named Belle. Where was it—Kansas City, Tombstone, Cheyenne—?

"Where's she now?"

"She married a miner from Dodge and went back East and she's a lady now. Wanted no truck with me, so I lit out."

"You stayed with her in Dodge?"

"Nah. That was in Abilene. I raised hell an' she told me to make tracks. Guess I was some headache to her, at that. She give me my bedroll and said to hit the road, so I did."

They reached the stable and turned. "The man's still there," Sean said.

"Yeah. I know. Followed me here. Name's Freeman, only I didn't expect him so soon."

"I'll get my gun."

"The hell you will!" Chagro exploded.

"Well, I wanted you to see it, anyway. Real accurate—I can pick a knob off a tree at two thousand yards. What's that man, Freeman, doggin' you for?"

He might as well have the rest of it, Chagro thought, straight out and flat and get it over with.

"Well, I stole some money, see? A robbery, and at the smell of cash, the vultures gather. There's a wanted out on me and these two others. A bank official an' the driver of the coach was killed in the fracas. I'm on the run."

"I know *that*. What's this Freeman after you for?"

Chagro's eyes widened. "The reward," he said softly. "Whole hog. And now you know."

"Don't make any difference," the kid sighed, "you're still my Pa. Just make things a little hotter, that's all. I'll get my gun."

This time Chagro let him go. He needed time to think, anyway. It wasn't every day a full grown son dropped into your life. Pa. He looked after the boy, who had retraced his steps, and through the rear stable door, he emerged carrying a rifle and pack.

Freeman had disappeared.

At thirteen, Altos Freeman had killed his first man, shot him in the back, and in the long and checkered career, there had been many more, one way and another. He was a smooth hand at cards and when that string played out, he turned bounty hunter. He'd hired on for a time with the cattleman's association, but the work was too tame for him. He took a job as shotgun guard for Wells Fargo but was implicated in a holdup, and he fled the immediate vicinity with a price on his head. That was five years ago up in California with the price still on his head. He'd changed his name—it was Martinson before—altered his appearance by growing longer hair and a beard, and again he faded, showing up inevitably where there were affairs to be settled by hired gun.

In his travels, Freeman had crossed the Irishman's trail in Kansas, in Utah, in the Nations, for the rollicking Brannigan's reputation was of the sort that preceded him, and everywhere Brannigan was well liked. Freeman continued to move southwest with the advancing march of civilization and its need for his kind.

He'd lit in Dos Brazos purely by accident and dismissing the place as the unfruitful backwater of nowhere was about to move on when Brannigan and the two others arrived on the scene; when events began popping, the hatchet-faced Freeman was there to be in on the kill. A coach loaded with money was tempting in the extreme and he'd considered it for himself, but it was no job for a man who, by the nature of his trade, worked alone. Habit was hard to break and Freeman above all was a creature of habit. A posse was a safer way of arriving at a goal, and it had worked out just as he wanted it to do.

Two weeks later, Freeman was still trying to trap his man. Not that there hadn't been opportunities, it was the overabundance of those opportunities that puzzled the gunman and turned him wary. This Brannigan walked open and free as though he hadn't a worry in the world. The Irishman evidently intended to sit it out until the time was right; there had to be some plan cooking in his head. Brannigan was different, Freeman decided, Brannigan was slick.

Haste had once near cost Freeman his life and lost him a chance at a fat reward, but it had made him a more painstaking hunter. Patience played a waiting game and an idea was beginning to jell. There was money buried in the hills somewhere and one of the three would lead him to it. That one, Freeman had already made up his mind, was Gault. He'd marked Gault's restlessness, the bitter impatience that rode him.

The deputy was here, too, and a kid sticking tighter to the Irishman than glue. Having been with the posse at the coach road, at the barranca during the ambush, Freeman figured it out. The particulars didn't concern him, save that the kid was a dead shot, had his father's interests obviously in mind, and was therefore to be reckoned with. Somehow the killing must be accomplished when the latter wasn't around to complicate the issue. Arresting was one thing and bounty was another. Bounty was where you found it.

Gunning down Brannigan presented no major problem, but properly handled, the coach money could be appropriated as well. With Brannigan and the Indian—he'd not forgotten the Indian— and the kid out of the way, Gault would be sole custodian of the cash. It seemed a fair guess the latter could be persuaded that thirty thousand was more to be desired than a mere ten thousand. Then Gault could be eliminated easily. With the loot cached safe for a later date, the world was his, Freeman's, for the taking.

Brannigan had a lot of friends in this town and clearly knew his way around, but Gault was still the weak link. Sooner or later, Gault would crack at the restraint and Freeman meant to be on hand to help it along. In all this Brannigan was the key figure, but man was a fragile thing; Brannigan was flesh and blood like anybody else and would die just as quick.

Freeman had never lacked confidence in himself.

Sean never went anywhere without his rifle. With an unexpected son, Chagro found his life more complicated than before. If he rode out, the kid rode with him unless ordered otherwise; if Brannigan entered the cantina for food or for drink, though the boy drank not at all, seeming not to like the stuff, he was to be found at Chagro's elbow.

Camargas was a sleepy little town where nothing much ever happened. A trio of rawhide characters rode in one night to look the village over, saw nothing worthwhile, and unaware of the drama brewing virtually under their noses, all rode out again. A herd of goats pattered through, and a mule train on its way to Yerros surfaced and remained several days, which was understandable, since most of its members were related to one or another of Camargas's citizens.

Akins walked the street's yellow dust and bided his time.

Annabelle Weems also bided her time but not so patiently. She saw Akins, Freeman, and came face to face with a lovely, stormy-eyed girl in the cantina one day. Chagro she couldn't catch up with and it was to her increasing frustration that she'd been able to catch a glimpse of him only from a distance, and only that once.

Exasperated, she presented herself at Guise House. "I want to see Chagro Brannigan."

"Who're you?"

It was not the answer Annabelle expected. She

drew herself up, scrabbling for her shreds of dignity under the huge woman's hardening stare.

"That doesn't matter! Is Mr. Brannigan here? I demand to see him."

"You *demand!*" The Guise seemed to swell even larger, her glance was thunderous. "Lady, nobody demands of me. Nobody! Understand? I've no one by that name on my books an' I wouldn't tell you if I did. If you want a room, say so fair an' square, an' I'm bettin' you will, since this's the only place in Camargas unless you want to bed down in the hay. I'll think it over. While I'm thinkin', you make up your mind. Then when you make up your mind, I'll think. That'll give us double time to get around the issue at hand." Madame tipped her head, seemed to weigh a further thought, and decided to lend it. "Wouldn't advise hangin' about on the streets at night though—no safe place for a woman. Even in a dusty little backwater like this, men get ideas. How long you been here?"

Annabelle's thin lips pinched tight and her cheeks flamed.

"Well, you're a wild one, ain't you?" Madame leered. "Come back in a couple hours, but I want one thing clear. I'm kind of particular 'bout gettin' in trouble with husbands an' men friends, so there'll be none of that in my house. Understood?"

Annabelle had flounced out, returned later, and was given a room, a stuffy, sparsely furnished, little cubicle she'd bet was the meanest the house afforded, just out of pure spite. Madame didn't like her, that was clear, and considered her an interloper. It was also clear that Madame was covering for Chagro Brannigan, which made Annabelle even more furious.

For the first time, she began to doubt the wisdom of coming along with Freeman, though coldness, she thought, forced Freeman to be a gentleman where she was concerned. She almost wished herself back in Dos Brazos.

The thought of Jefferson was beginning to bother her, too, not out of any pinch of conscience, but because of what he would do when he did catch up. How could she explain, without certain admissions, that she'd come to see Brannigan brought to his knees for flouting her? That if there was some way out, of retiring gracefully and still saving face, she'd jump at it? Annabelle thought a good deal about saving face, unaware of how little others cared.

Raised by an indulgent mother and a doting aunt, she'd grown up with the notion that the world not only owed her its best but its obeisance as well. That events were not working out quite along those lines was becoming increasingly clear, which was worrying her now.

Stepping out of the hotel one morning, she was to come face to face again with the girl she'd confronted before. Annabelle drew back. "What do you want?"

"Come behind the building. I like to talk to you."

*Mexican*, Annabelle's contempt said, and her lips curled. "Why should I? We don't know each other and you can have nothing to say that I want to hear."

Pilar's head jerked. "In back. Now. You come, eh?"

Something in the girl's attitude forced Annabelle to do her bidding; a ripple of fear scratched Annabelle's nerves.

"You know what I am going to tell you? It is a warning. I think you know what about."

Annabelle flared, "What can it matter to me what you have to tell? You're nothing but an ignorant—" and attempted to flip past. A competently outthrust toe and Annabelle went flat.

She came up raging and blowing dust. "Why, you—" and rushed at the other. Pilar stepped aside. In the furious onslaught, Pilar caught a handful of Annabelle's wiry, red hair and nearly ripped it from her head. Again Annabelle went down.

It drew a few bystanders. Shocked and recognizing the participants, Sean galloped for Chagro. "Pa, there's two females in a hair-pullin' match behind the hotel! Come quick!"

Chagro ambled over. "Aren't you going to stop 'em?" the boy urged.

"What for?" Chagro stood, thumbs hooked in his belt, and watched the dust boil. "You got a lot to learn, boy. Never step in between two warrin' women. Besides, I haven't had so much fun since my Dad kicked the soda can over in the biscuits."

"No ladies'd act that way," snorted Sean. "Whoever started it—and I'm bettin it was that firebox Pilar—ain't no lady."

Chagro lifted one and the next moment Sean found himself measuring his length in the dirt.

"If there's one thing I can't abide, it's a lippy

kid," Chagro observed through set teeth.

"But I ain't had no man to raise me, Pa—"

"Well, you got one now! And don't forget it. Let this be a lesson."

The kid got up slowly, rubbing his jaw. Infinite respect was in his eyes. And admiration but some puzzlement, too.

"And be careful who you're callin' no lady, see?"

The boy nodded; his eyes sought the dark-skinned Pilar and light commenced to dawn. "Yeah, Pa, I sure will, Pa."

The fight had ended and Pilar triumphantly rearranged her skirts; Annabelle fled to the hotel in disgrace.

"She really broke away, didn't she?" an aged and graveled voice said behind Chagro and the latter turned. He studied the rheumy, wise, old eyes, the seamed face cracked in a grin. The grin held.

"Grimshaw?" Brannigan said carefully.

"The same. Long ways from Dos Brazos, ain't it? Didn't recall it was quite so fur. My bones won't stand many more such trips. Damn shakin' mule-back. I'm a mule man myself, howsomever."

Chagro's gaze had slipped down over the old one and saw no star. Akins was enough and Akins was here. What did Grimshaw come for?

"You take this Pa business real serious, don't you?" the old man said.

"Well, when a man gets a late start, there's nothin' like catchin' up." Chagro took a deep breath, straightened, suddenly smiled. "Buy you a drink," he said.

# NINE

Seated across from Grimshaw, Chagro began it. "Look, we could buck and fill for awhile and waste a lot of time, but that's not my way. So I'll come right out with it. What you here for?"

Grimshaw rolled his drink flavorfully beneath his tongue, swallowed it, and sighed. "Figgered there'd be some action. Man, I ain't had any for so long I forget what it's like. It's makin' me old, an' when a fella starts lettin' hisself feel thataway, he's done. Ready for the boneyard. Well, it just occurred to me I wasn't, yet. I was with the posse in Matagordo, Dawson s'posed to meet us there but didn't, so we figgered there was no use stickin' around an' went back to Dos Brazos. Then we found out why he didn't show up. Sheriff was dead—just tipped from his hoss, dead when he hit the ground. Franks brung the word, said Akins been deputized to take after you. With Dawson gone, guess that makes 'im full sheriff. The town voted on it. Voted unanimous."

"Sure he'll be glad to know that," grunted Chagro. "And now let's hear about you."

The old man's bony shoulders lifted. "I ain't after you or nobody. Got no axe to grind, couldn't if I wanted to. It's just like I tell you—I wanted a little stirrin' up before plantin' time an' I aimed me here as the best place to do it."

"You trailed me?"

"Yeah. Used to be a scout with Fremont. Been across the east-west paths so many times they're printed on my eyeballs. Still don't do so bad if I say so myself, only takes me a little longer. Akins here?"

"Around."

"Figgered he would be." Grimshaw removed his hat, scrubbed his fringe of hair, replaced the hat, then added sympathetically, "If he's a friend of yours, he ain't goin' to like this."

Chagro didn't reply to the statement, he asked only, "The rest of 'em with you?"

Grimshaw snorted. "What rest? Ain't no rest to it. No, I'm alone. Still wary of me, ain't you? Well, in your place I'd feel the same. But you got no call to itch. I wouldn't drag nobody down here, if they was to come, they'd come alone. I ain't playin' nursemaid no more, not to you nor nobody else. Freeman didn't come back, so I figgered he was down here, Akins didn't, so he was. If they's goin' to be fireworks, I aim to be in on 'em, is all, even if it's as a bystander, though," he added wistfully, "sure would admire to limber up Old Betsy just once more." Grimshaw gestured to his hip. "Used to do all right by her, too. Well, you take it from there.''

Chagro thought of Akins, of Freeman, and most of all, of Freeman. And that damned woman—he could almost laugh. Spice and rawhide. They'd settled their differences all right, Pilar with the fight in her fist all the way. Some girl, he thought, Pilar was some girl.

There was a stir at the door and Sean peered in. ''Want something?''

''No, just wondering where you was. I thought if you wasn't real busy, me 'n you might do a little target shooting, is all. You promised.''

Grimshaw chuckled. ''Minds me of my brother's kid. Guess he's got you pegged. Well, good luck.''

''Bit off a big bite but you know something?'' Chagro said as he rose, ''Not all of it's sour. Either that or I'm beginnin' to get used to it. Guess we were through here anyway. Help yourself to the bottle.''

Later Chagro spoke idly to the Seminole in the shadows of the stable wall. His cigarette described an arc. ''Nice out tonight.''

''Nice out every night,'' the Indian murmured. ''I like the dry smell of earth.''

''Not like the swamps of Florida where you grew up. Listen to the crickets. Good things everywhere if you open your eyes an' ears to take 'em in. Ever sorry you left?''

''A boy grows up enough, he likes to roam, he makes up his mind he has to see over the next hill. No, I've not regretted going. This country pleases me.'' The Seminole tipped his head to a coyote calling to its mate—a long, rippling appeal in the darkness. "Lonesome sound," he said, "that's how it seems to us. But ever think of it another way? A lot can be read into the lovesick cry of a brush-walloper."

"And you of the open spaces," Chagro said. "You should have been born a gentleman."

"Each of us is born so," the Indian said quietly. He had never spoken of his past life and did not elaborate now. "It is only what a man does to himself later that soils him." He paused, then added, "We stand and wait until the train goes by?"

Chagro threw his cigarette away, leaving the question unanswered. They turned and moved by common consent to the side door entry of Madame Guise's and let themselves downstairs. Chagro lighted a candle and when they were seated, he shoved over the bottle. The Indian waved it away and Chagro poured for himself. Then he said, "Nothing like it. We stand an' wait until the train comes."

"Ah," the Seminole breathed, "I see. I gather, though, you have not said this to our partner. I have seen Dutch talking to the bounty hunter when they thought no one was watching."

Chagro permitted himself a brief chuckle. "He can have what's left when the party's over, if he'd rather have it that way. Did you get near enough to hear what they were saying?"

"No, only that Dutch seemed to have complaints and the bounty hunter was agreeing with him. A mess cooks over that fire, I think, that does not smell so good. Pretty soon we will have the whole of Dos Brazos here, and then the town will have increased in size. This worries me. You walk too broadly and openly. And now Grimshaw, merely an old man, but another to get in the way. Soon also I suppose the husband of the red-haired woman."

"Not yet for awhile." Chagro explained; Grimshaw had dropped the word that Weems was roaring to leave Dos Brazos but hadn't yet done so when Grimshaw pulled out. Knotted up with one or another of his businesses, Grimshaw supposed.

"How did you decide this other?"

"Easy. Look," Chagro said. "The time of the rains down here is along in June and July, right? There's good mesas in the hills southeast of this place and the first grass is always best. A mule outfit started by normal traveling will reach the mesas by the time of the first grass. They do it every year. An' one of 'em will be carrying a church bell—mine."

Even the Indian had trouble with this one. The big Irishman's thoughts moved cleverly, yet in simple lines. So simple as to be misinterpreted, the Seminole thought admiringly. His own thoughts picked up the trail. "These mesas. They would be south and east of El Paso and almost due south of Isleta. And who would notice just another dusty mule train? It could get a good head start. And the bell, it goes to—?"

"Friends," admitted Chagro, and showed some embarrassment. "Well, the first thing they think of is a church—you know? Folks set great store by them in these little Mex villages, a matter of prestige." Chapel bells, he thought. Sounded nice. And tiny Isleta had no bell. A steeple but no bell. He'd looked back leaving Isleta and noticed that. He added, trying to explain, "I owe for a long time, see? Maybe this will catch it up. A bell rings 'em in, rings 'em out if they got one. If they don't, they're only half married. Be the pride of the countryside."

The Seminole shook his head. "Because a mule train is Mexican and traveling to the mesas does not mean it is safe, even if it carries a church bell. I have heard bandits flourish in the area."

"A chance we have to take, a chance they take any time they go across that country. The bell has nothing to do with it except as a gift—but here's the rest of what you wanted to know; if twenty mules come in, twenty-two will leave, if thirty-six come, thirty-eight will leave. Who cares? *Vaya con Dios.* If that bell decides to put in a good word for us along the way, so much the better. We'll wait and see about that."

"But," the Indian asked, "where is a bell to be found? I have not seen a loose one in all of my travels, nor in Camargas."

"Send out word and you get a ripple," the Irishman suggested. "Got one coming, it'll be here in time. Don't worry about that part of it."

"And how do you plan to get away? Have you thought that out yet?"

"One way straight. Make a run for it. Diversion would help, or just some dark night when the time is right. What's on my mind is Freeman. It's my guess he's cozying up to Dutch with an eye to the

110

big rakeoff. He's not after me personally anymore, I only stand in the way. With us out of the picture, that leaves only Dutch. And with Dutch some on the stupid side and mad enough, it'll go the way Freeman steers it. That leaves nobody to tell the tale, that leaves Freeman in the clear with a pocketful of dollars.''

"What about Sean?"

Chagro frowned. "I only hope to hell when the time comes, he keeps out of the way. I want him out of the way too for another reason, because I'm crowdin' Freeman. I'm makin' it so damn easy he can't pass me up—I don't want all the bullets flying at the same time if I can help it. I don't plan on exactly setting myself up as a target, but he'll make the first move."

"Akins—what about Akins?"

"He'll keep out of it, he'll have to. He'd like to get his hands on that money for the law's sake, but he won't even know when it's gone or for awhile, how, if I can manage it."

The Indian had an absolutely smooth face that rarely showed emotion and a pair of light blue eyes that most found disconcerting, but bothered Chagro not at all. It occurred to him that the eyes' color was an infusion of white blood somewhere along the line, but he had never asked. The Indian was smiling now, thoroughly pleased and showing that pleasure.

"You dissipate my bad thoughts," he said. "I owe you my life and I'll give it if I have to, but for a long time I have seen only darkness, as though none of us would get out of this alive, as though it

111

was all going to end right here in this little place, or not far from it. Now I believe differently. I feel you are right and that there is a brighter day coming. But for us to get away—I did not know about that. Now as I say, I feel better."

Chagro had looked at him sharply, now he shrugged. "Where do thoughts begin and where do they end? You think too much. Not good for the digestion."

Had he laid his plans right? Chagro sought the darkness of the porch, considering. There was only one way to get the gold out, so far as he could see. One safe way. The Mexican drover, Carlos, and his helpers wanted to do it for nothing, out of friendship, out of enthusiasm for the forbidden, for the underdog. Whatever, Chagro decided it wouldn't be for nothing. All had homes and families, and if some of the bank's gold became scattered between here and Isleta, so much the better.

A bulk moved up out of the dark. "Pa? You all through talkin'? I been waitin' till you was all through talkin' in there. I had to see you."

"What's up?" Chagro's tone was guarded.

Sean lowered his voice. "Well, I heard something. These two men talking, the one you call Dutch Gault, and Freeman. I followed 'em and they're still there. I think, if we hurry—" He laid a hand on his father's arm and pulled him into the darkness.

There was a feed store of ancient wood and adobe, long abandoned, and at the far end of the street, a string of tumbledown thatch and mud shacks; treading debris, the boy stopped at the end one to press against the wall. Brannigan stepped close, his eyes locating the small shine of a candle from within.

Dutch Gault, with no care at all, sat with his back to the door; Freeman observed more caution and was so stationed as to permit him to see both the door and the single window.

Gault was raging. "By God, I knew it! Tomorrow I'm goin to lay it before the bastard, then I'm goin' to kill him! He's got away with it right under our noses somehow. Pretty God damned cute, sneakin' behind my back, a little too damn cute! I'll make 'im wish—"

"Shut up," the gunman said coldly, evenly. "You'll do nothing of the sort because the minute you open your mouth, he'll know you been snooping around. For what reason? You've caught the scent of trouble and it's made you wild. A man off his hook can't think. Now think. How could Brannigan do it? He hasn't had any chance to get away with it, he's been here or right around here all the time. We'd known if he had."

"Well, it's gone!"

"Keep your voice down!" Freeman snapped. "Want the whole world to hear you?" He stepped lightly to the door, stood a moment listening outside, then withdrew to take up his former watchful station. "Damned loot's got to be somewhere," the gunman pointed out. "If it's not, you're no good to me anymore, don't forget that. Remember our agreement?"

"Why, you sneakin' son-of-a—"

There was a sharp click. "Don't try it," Freeman retorted. "You're in my sights and I'm twice as fast. I could cut you in two before you could touch your gun. Now there's no sense in us fighting. Just hold your temper and everything will be all right. If Brannigan's moved that money, it's up to you to find out where, that's all. You've got the inside track, it shouldn't be hard. You're still a partner. One thing I'd like to know is where he goes. He rides out almost every day with that kid, exercising the horse, target shooting, or just riding. One direction one time, another the next, never takes anything with him or brings anything back. I can't figure it."

Gault seemed to have regained his bravado. "Well, you made yourself boss man," he grunted sourly, "you better figger it. Smart or dead. We ain't goin' to play this string long before Brannigan gets wise. Force it out of him, is my advice. Hit 'im, hit 'im just right an' start 'im bleedin' good, then screw the truth out, make 'im tell where he's hid it. I'm damn tired of waitin' for this break you're always talkin' about."

"There's something here I don't quite understand," murmured Freeman and for the first time, there was doubt in the tone. "It's Brannigan. I catch myself sometimes—never mind. The sooner this thing comes to a head, the better it suits me, too. He gets in my craw—"

Chagro pulled away from the wall. Sean followed, and together they made their way carefully from the danger zone, through the back alleys, and to the street. In a building's deep shadow, Chagro halted, the kid near piling up behind him.

"Nice to catch up on what's been goin' on behind your back," Chagro stated ominously. "Now let's have it and, by God, it better be straight. You had something to do with this—you knew what we were goin' to hear?"

"Well, yes, sir, I had a idea, that is—I thought we might. Guess I'm in trouble again."

"Yeah?"

"Well, I did it. I moved it, see—"

"You *what?*"

"Moved it to a better place because I figured—I was pretty sure what Gault and Freeman were up to. Once I really thought Gault was goin' to make the break all by himself. You know that rock knob—"

"Not here," Chagro said grimly. "For Christ's sake, not here. You daft? Come on."

# TEN

All that week and the next and well into June, Chagro walked lightly and carefully. The bell arrived, and the first mule string padded through the village headed for the mesas.

Little Camargas was waking up, an awakening consistent each year with the arrival and departures of animals destined for richer pastures to the north and east. The next train would take the bell, the Seminole would accompany it, then drop it off and wait for Chagro. A third train would bypass Camargas entirely and with that one would go the gold.

Talk was around town that there might be a contingent of military showing up one of these days, a rumor Chagro hoped unfounded, but it would not surprise him.

Leaks came easy in an operation like this. Somebody got wind of money and passed the word; for personal glory or personal gain, some diligent enough to claim it for Mexico because it was on

Mexican soil. Others, even those in service of their government, were not above taking it unto themselves. Wealth was to the strong, or to the clever.

Dutch Gault was abusive and argumentative by turns and increasingly vicious. In a drunken brawl, he shot and wounded a man whose brother-in-law—almost everybody was related in Camargas—had threatened to carve out his liver and would have done so, had not Chagro intervened.

In all of this, Chagro managed to keep the lid on, giving Gault sufficient rope to hang himself if he were so minded, yet passing no more information than was actually necessary. For Dutch was no longer to be trusted. He was mushy—going bad. Goaded by Freeman, he'd become a bot-stung bull, red eyed and pawing for the kill.

Now that the escape plan was established, every detail must be worked out very carefully so when the time came, everything would go off smoothly and without a hitch.

Then there was Sean. Chagro never had been entirely in favor of leaving him behind and was less so now. He'd have to be in on it, there was no other way. Either that or he'd be clawing at the trail forever after. Anyhow, what man could do such a stunt, knowing he had a son? Even at this point, Chagro recognized tenacity and something else that made him ashamed for entertaining such an idea. No, the boy must be told, square and straight across, before he took some damn, fool notion of his own and made a mess of things.

He had found a good place for the money, all

117

right. There was a cleft that from the ground resembled no cleft at all, and upward for a space of twenty yards or so, a ridge whose sides pinched in to form a watershed—when there was water—and still farther, safe above this in a ragged tumble of boulders were twin rocks whose overhang formed a natural, stone-lined depression. This was the niche he'd chosen.

It was a mystery how he managed to get up to it in the first place, big as he was, let alone secrete a canvas bag. Only an act of God would ever unearth it, Chagro thought, but damn the kid anyway. He should be taught to keep his mitts off things that didn't concern him. Still, Chagro owned to a sense of frustration not unmixed with wonder. Seemed most things the kid did turned out right. This situation, for instance. He'd only meant to protect the money; even Chagro had to admit that with an itchy-fingered Gault on the prod, the sum might be too great a temptation to resist.

And standing alone on the porch in the dusk, Chagro had to chuckle. From now on crowd him, crowd the kid, that was the way. Somehow he felt it in his bones.

From a vantage point a few doorways down, Dan Akins had observed that big figure, saw the figure step to the street, and make its way toward the well where a girl was drawing water. She had one olla full and was filling another and looked up as Chagro approached. The girl—it was Pilar—laughed low in her throat, left her ollas and came forward, hips swinging and both hands out-stretched.

Absorbed in this little byplay, Akins nearly overlooked a shadow that moved stealthily at the building side. Akins's shouted warning was simultaneous with the orange flame that stabbed the deeper dark, this almost in conjunction with Chagro's own shot, fired from the hip as he leaped for the safety of the well's stone curb, pulling the girl down with him. There was no third shot. Footsteps pelted down an alley and faded.

"You all right?" It was Akins's voice.

"Yeah." Chagro rose and holstered his gun as Akins came up. Chagro had the girl shoved protectively behind him. One olla was smashed; that's how close it was.

*"Mira!"* she cried and gestured angrily. "Look at that!" A pedestrian had ducked immediately for the doorway, crying out the alarm. A mule screamed in fright and there was commotion over at the hitch rack and a string of six animals, recently tied there, broke free to plunge for the street, neck and neck, churning up clouds of dust in their passage.

Chagro had left Sean playing checkers with old man Grimshaw, but now the boy boiled out of the cantina, looking wildly up and down the street.

"Go on back," Chagro yelled. "Everything's all right—hear? Some mescal-happy pilgrim shootin' loose. Go on back, I say." Sean faded, reluctantly.

"Who was it?" Chagro asked. "You see him?"

"I don't know," Akins replied. "Couldn't tell much there in the shadow and it happened so fast. Somebody short an' stocky though, I think, a Mex. You ought to be more careful. Missed that time,

119

might not the next. Only takes one bullet."

"That is what I keep telling him!" interposed the girl; Chagro ignored her.

His tone was unusually subdued. "What would you suggest?"

"You know damn well what I'd suggest!" Akins exploded. "I've spelled it out before. You're not stupid an' you're not reckless in some things, not where your life is concerned, but you're pushin' your luck. You walk a narrow line an' dare yourself to fall off. You—" Akins quit on this, aware that Chagro was not listening. "Ah," Akins growled, "forget it. My turn—buy you a drink."

"No. No, thanks. You run along," Chagro instructed the girl, "I got some thinkin' to do." The big man turned away, then paused and swung back. "Thanks, Dan," he said quietly. "I owe you one. Maybe more than one."

The episode seemed to have kicked the sand from under Chagro's feet and Akins looked after him in amazement.

A half dozen strangers, Indios and Mex, had drifted in and tied up in Camargas last night. Long before they hit town, Chagro was advised of their coming and assured himself upon their arrival that he knew none of them. Who was after his scalp? It could be anybody. Approached by Freeman, by Dutch Gault, or maybe something somebody heard on the trail and brought with him. A thousand dollar reward was sufficient inducement in itself to spark a character to great and incredible deeds. A thousand was more than most men saw in a lifetime, more than many in two lifetimes. Where a border was more a word on men's lips than an actual boundary, the fine points of the law meant little. Some would attempt it. And with a target in plain sight—Chagro owned he'd made one. A king on his throne, he thought ruefully, takes only one brick to topple him, or like Dan said, only one bullet.

It could happen any time. Chagro had faced it all before but never with the seriousness that struck him now. He'd never refused a challenge or run from a fight, but with the insouciance of a happy-go-lucky man, he failed to plumb the deeper implications.

Death had brushed him by many times and would again. He wasn't afraid of that, but now for the first time he wondered, to what end was he dragging other people?

Pilar, she'd take the bumps, such was the girl's loyalty. And Sean. Yes, and now Sean. What about the boy? Was this any kind of sentence for him? He deserved better. The kid would stick clear to hell and back, Chagro knew that, too. Sean had no easy time so far—what was he, Pa, Dad, doing to better it? At this point, what *could* he do?

Chagro stared up toward the dark cliffs beyond the town and wrestled with his foreign thoughts, and sweat. It was like being in a river, keep paddling or go under. For some time he stood thus to chase his worries about, and at last, like Akins, swore fervently, "Ah, hell," and turned inside.

The cantina was dim and smoke filled and humid from the day's trapped heat. There was laughter, the clink of glasses, and in an alcove off

121

the main room, a stolid waitress carried trays of chili and tortillas; this and the slabbed beef and the huge sweet Spanish onions made up most of the menu.

Chagro looked over the crowd briefly, seeing in a far corner, bent over a table and ostensibly over a game, Freeman and Dutch Gault; engrossed as they were, neither saw him. Alone at the end of the bar, turned so as to watch the two at the table, the Seminole idly nursed a glass; he raised his head and lifted a hand to Chagro.

The newcomers, the mule men, had vacated the place in pursuit of their animals. Chagro moved to the rail and when the bartender came, said, "Know those fellows in here earlier, the ones that just busted out—ever see any of 'em before?"

The bartender shook his head. "They come, they go. Rough ones, eh? My guess are bandidos. Out in the hills, who knows? I would not say it where they could hear it, though." The bartender made a graphic slicing motion across his throat and shrugged. "Eight, nine years ago, many such come and hold the town in fear. Kill, rob. Then they go—soldiers come, they run. I theenk these go too—nothing here for them."

"Already gone," Chagro suggested lightly. "Thanks," and added, "seen the lawman around?"

"*Senor* Akins? *Si.*" The other gestured. "In the dining room you fin' him, I think."

Chagro thumbed back his hat and slipped into a vacant chair opposite Dan Akins.

"What you going to do about the badge, Sheriff?" Chagro indicated Akins's chest.

122

Akins had looked up, measured the other, and now shook his head, frowning. "You might know. Resign, of course. When I get back to civilization, I'm goin' to be a free man again, you can bet my bottom dollar on that. I'm a farmer, not a lawman. Full sheriff or flunky, I never wanted the job in the first place an' I don't cotton to it bein' wished on me. You're my last hope. Sure you won't consider?"

"Beans look good."

"Tell that to the cook," Akins grunted sourly, "don't tell it to me." A puzzled Akins had waited and watched. He had scoured the hills himself and found nothing, and the Irishman wasn't going to crack. Chagro had made no questionable move, no move at all. He seemed perfectly content to while away the days gaming, drinking with his friends, sitting all night, many nights, over poker tables at Madame Guise's, with others in the cantina, with the youth or with various girls, generally Pilar if she managed to cut the others out, and she was good at that. Pilar might have the inside track or she might not—there was a blonde over at Madame Guise's and you never could tell about Chagro. The Irishman loved 'em all.

For Akins, the thought of home pulled hard. He felt he should be there and wanted to be, but having come this far, he knew he couldn't quit now. There seemed no way to break the deadlock. Chagro was waiting for something, that was clear.

"Billy will be glad to see you again," suggested Chagro as if reading his mind. "When you leaving?"

"Did I say I was leaving?" Akins squinted up from beneath his brows. "You look like the cat that ate the canary. What's up?"

"The cat that choked on the canary," Chagro Brannigan suggested." I been reviewin' my sins."

"And—?"

"Decided to continue in 'em," said Chagro cheerfully. "What else? The hungry ones come sniffin'."

"Yeah to that. A few get killed an' a few walk away. What's Billy goin' to think?"

Chagro winced. "Don't tell 'im. Carrie either. Let it go and after awhile they'll forget, especially Billy. I'd like to give him something though, maybe something real fine. I could get—"

"Think that's a good idea?"

"No. Maybe not." Chagro's face settled, a look of almost sadness touched it and was gone. He grinned. "Don't waste your worry on me, though. I'll be busy, diggin' out my own little niche."

"More likely your grave," muttered Akins. "You're stubborn, bullheaded, an' I oughtn't to bother with you. I don't know why I do! Except it's a waste of a good man. You got an enterprisin' head on your shoulders, you could be anything you wanted to be, but will you? You go cocky on me every time I get on the subject. Won't nothin' I say change your mind? The cards are all against you, you're buckin' a stacked deck an' can't win. When're you pullin' out?"

Brannigan's eyes twinkled. "Didn't know I was," he drawled. "The sermon better be about over, here comes your grub." From the corner of

124

his eye, he marked movement—Freeman and Gault were leaving, Freeman glancing into the dining room to pin down Chagro's presence as he passed. Nothing much escaped the gunman. "Just as a matter of curiosity," Chagro wanted to know, "what became of Jeff Weems's wife?"

"You haven't heard? She started out with a party, a Mex woman an' all the relations headed north to visit the family up in Sonora, promised 'em good pay to take her to the border, but they got chased back by Indians. Made it by the skin of their teeth. If she ain't careful, she's goin' to be right here where she didn't want to be when Jeff comes roarin' in."

"I think she has not so much red hair as before," Pilar remarked, coming up beside them. "I will take that," she said to the waitress and lifted the food and placed it before Akins.

She sat down, elbows on the tabletop and the black gaze roving Chagro warmly. Hoop earrings twinkled, once again the smooth, brown shoulders were nearly bare, the ruffled blouse slipped low. "Where is your plate?" she demanded. "You better eat, keep strength up for the big fight."

The Irishman winked at her, at Akins. "What big fight?"

Pilar's eyes flashed, she leaned close and whispered. *"That* big fight." Her head jerked, setting the earrings in motion. "Maybe you already know, eh? Then you know what these two plan, that Gault and that Freeman. And this old man, this innocent old man, he's goin' get hurt."

Chagro alerted at once. "What old man—

125

Grimshaw? What's he got to do with it?"

The girl shrugged, she straightened. "I hear him say he know this man Freeman, the one with the look of a killer upon him. We not wait till we see what they got in mind, huh?"

"Look," Chagro ordered sternly and pinned both her wrists in a firm grip, "you stay out of this, hear? When you figure you got a say in such things, I quit. Understand? Pass the word but don't take it any, farther. I don't like hornin'-in women."

Pilar suddenly slipped from his grasp, laughing in a pleased sort of way. *"Si,"* she said, "you win. Not like the Annabelle, eh? Or Dolly—or any of them. Mr. Deputy Akins, you my witness—this Chagro Brannigan ask marry me, I say sure you bet. By God, yes, any time you ready."

Akins choked, set down his coffee cup. "Pinned back your ears that time," he said.

"Hey," Chagro protested, "wait a minute. Just hold on! Maybe some day but not now. I'll come back after you, all right? Anyway, here's no place to hash over private matters."

Days passed and Chagro continued to ride out as was his custom. On this particular day he gave the horse his head and presently became aware of someone following him. It was Freeman; even at a considerable distance the long, taut figure could be identified as the gunman. Freeman hadn't seen him.

A small, cold smile of satisfaction touched Chagro's lips; he swung around a thicket of scrub

126

oak and paloverde and quickly dismounted.

A dry branch, long since denuded of leaves, tested a certain hiding place to find no evidence of snakes; from the hole was retrieved an object created of burlap and stuffed with hay to resemble a man, a hat of sorts added to complete the illusion and the object bound to the saddle—the deception all passable from afar. Then with the horse headed out in what was shortly to be full view of the gunman, Chagro settled down to wait.

A bee sailed overhead, and cicadas, briefly disturbed by human intrusion, resumed their communal song. It was near noon, a brassy sun blazed straight down and it was very hot.

Freeman came on, then identifying the horse and perceiving the figure aboard it, immediately swerved to one side and pulled up. Then he coolly hauled a rifle from the boot and levered in a shell.

It happened fast. There was no word, no called-out warning. With the scarecrow's back turned to him, Freeman simply leveled and fired. One minute the horse was placid, the next plunged in fright as the straw figure toppled from its perch.

Freeman stiffened with shock as he realized he had been duped. Then all in one swift motion, he stowed the rifle and filled his fist with a sixgun, whirling about to confront any hidden marksman.

Some time before, old Grimshaw had observed Freeman's departure from town. He had moved out purposefully and now confronted the gunman. Grimshaw was afoot.

Freeman's horse shied at that small and erect and almost comic figure planted in its path. "Get out of my way, you crazy old coot! What's the matter with you?"

"I ain't movin'."

Freeman dismounted, he towered over the oldster.

The seamed face turned upward. "I know you, Martinson. A lot of folks know you, especially sheriffs. I been thinkin' I knowed you from someplace—was a'most sure of it in Brazos, am sure of it now. Out in Californy, wasn't it? About five years ago. A reward out, a good one. You was—"

Freeman's hand streaked, his revolver roared; the old man hadn't time to hoist his own weapon clear of the leather. A red explosion blew half his chest away and he dropped, first buckling at the knees, then crumpled like an old sack to the ground.

*"Freeman!"* A first wild yell was lost in the crash of gunfire, the second rose behind Freeman, and he spun but too late. It was Chagro Brannigan he was facing, and all that coolness deserted him as he saw the livid flare in Brannigan's eyes and the destruction that blazed there for him. He saw it and flung a shot that went wild. Chagro's bullet caught him and spun him half around in a macabre dance of death, and he pitched forward on his face, his hand, empty now of any weapon at all. In this last act, he fell across the heap of rags and old bones that was Grimshaw.

In battle, soldiers often died while still on their feet, were known to have squeezed off bullets to cut down an adversary after all sense and life had fled. God only knew what went through men's minds at certain times or why they did what they did. It was a fool stunt, bracing a professional like Freeman but done now, and no retreat. Never any retreat.

Chagro hesitated but a moment. He caught up the old man's gun and pressed it into the gnarled fist to carefully and deliberately fire the shot that would go down in remembrance as the fast—and final—triumph of Old Betsy.

# ELEVEN

Akins roused late, certainly late for him, whose habit it was to rise before the sun, and scratched and yawned to full wakefulness. There'd been a double wedding last night at Guise House, with even more mescal than usual, and he had to admit he'd succumbed happily before the first hitch was over—not his usual style at all. Once in a blue moon he slid over the edge and this was one of those times.

Chagro was in and out, the happiest of the lot, and they'd bent convivial elbows together in celebration of the momentous event. In the feast that followed, Akins had not been an active participant, his last remembrance of a grinning face and a big fist—not Chagro's—that thrust still another glass into his outstretched hand. After that, both festivities and revelers became something of a blur.

He had a mouth that felt like fuzz and a thirst for more of the hair of the dog that bit him. Breakfast at the cantina consisting of tortillas and black coffee, and leave off the tortillas, was what he'd get, and somehow the day would start.

Somebody had thoughtfully managed him upstairs and put him to bed, for he was peeled down to underwear and socks. His hat was on the stand beside a water jug, pants and gunbelt carefully hung over the head of the bed, boots on the floor—the boots cleaned and polished, by God! When these Mexicans did things, they really did 'em up proper.

He eased to sitting position, wincing. Never knew mescal to have such a kick, but of course if you got enough of it down—

It was quiet around the place, real quiet. Nice to sleep. He looked back at the bed and gave up the notion, mentally regretting. A good thing could go on only so long and he had things to do, though at the moment he couldn't recall exactly what.

Akins stood up, testing his legs, then carefully walked to the window. The street was deserted. The whole town must have laid one on. Some blowout. The Mex knew how to celebrate, too. Never saw people throw themselves into partying more wholeheartedly.

Deep shadows between the buildings startled him at first. It had to be late, later than he thought. How long was it since he'd slept the clock around? A string of something dangled from his hair and he shook it off—a shred of paper streamer—the movement rattled his head and he winced again. He reached the bed, eased on his hat, and climbed into his pants. By the time he had finished

131

dressing, he felt better.

It was late all right, late afternoon, and the dining room was empty. The bar had its few customers, but Dutch Gault was not among them. If Gault wasn't in the cantina drinking himself into blind fury, he'd be out picking fights, favorite pasttimes now that Freeman was out of the picture. Gault was bad medicine and men let him strictly alone. The Seminole was nowhere about either. Come to think of it, he hadn't seen the Seminole around the last few days, but you never saw much of the Seminole anyway. Quiet fellow, kind of drifted in and out and made no ripples at all.

Akins ordered and ate, surprised to find he was hungry. Even the coffee, thick as mud and black as night, tasted good. Briefly he wondered where Brannigan and the kid had got to. Off target shooting probably, they were most always together. Funny how a kid could look like two shovelsful less than a load, yet be so sharp. Except in some situations, he was still bumbling but he was young yet. Likely a dead ringer for his Dad at that age, though with a little of the devilment watered out. And Chagro was good company, always had been that. Hell with the hide off and never knowing which way he'd jump, but good company nonetheless. Knowing his own family, Carrie and Billy, Akins knew also that Chagro, whatever the circumstances, would be welcome in their home anytime.

Dan Akins had long envied Chagro Brannigan his ease with others but couldn't emulate it. The big fellow liked people, laughter, music; he drank with them, swapped stories with them, played poker, and goodnaturedly fought for them at the drop of a hat. Couldn't beat him out with a gun either, the Irishman was the fastest Akins ever saw, and he did it with a flair, with a laugh, as he did everything else. But not the Grimshaw-Freeman business. It was pretty clear to Akins that Brannigan had baited Freeman, knowing the latter to be a troublemaker, and when the gunman drew down on the old man, Brannigan shot him. That wasn't what most would believe, or what Brannigan wanted them to believe, but Akins knew Chagro Brannigan and in a like position, he would have done the same himself. Justice moved quickly in this rough land as it did above the border, and a man settled his differences in a way he knew best.

Akins looked around. Funny Camargas was so dead even at this hour of late afternoon, but that was the way it went. Jumping one day with the arrival of a train, asleep the next with its departure. The last outfit went through—when was it? He couldn't remember but there probably wouldn't be another for about a week. The traffic was beginning to dribble off.

Akins finished his coffee, ordered a second cup, and when it came, drank that. The waitress shuffled in to light the candles in both rooms; a cricket that had taken up residence in a dank corner behind the tables commenced to chirp.

Akins listened to these things, took them all in, and unease rippled along his nerves. It was quiet—

too quiet, as though waiting for him to start something. Prodded by that sense of unease, he got to his feet and leaving the price of the meal on the table, walked quickly into the outer area. The bartender was nowhere in sight but a small man, a Mexican Akins didn't know, rose from a table at the rear of the room and came forward.

"*Senor* Deputy Akins? I have here sometheeng for you, a note from *Senor* Brannigan." He extended a folded paper.

"Brannigan!" Akins swore and faced down that unease, knowing now the cause of it. The paper crackled in his fingers, the scrawled message was in a handwriting he recognized:

> *So long, old son. Sure hated to leave without saying goodbye but you was sleeping so peaceful I didn't have the heart to wake you up. A word of advice: watch that spiked mescal. See you sometime and take care of yourself.*
>
> *Chagro.*

Akins swore again, furiously. "Why in hell didn't you get this to me before? I been sitting right in there!"

The Mexican shrugged, the smile never wavered. "*Senor* Chagro say give to you when you happy. When a man eat he happy. So I wait till you happy."

"When did he go—which way did he go?"

Another shrug; he'd get nothing out of the man. There was no use to try. Akins whirled and bolted from the place. Outside in the street, he stared up and down, still cursing himself for being a fool. Nothing, of course. What had he expected? Chagro was miles away by now. When had he left? Akins racked his brain. It was Chagro at the party, wasn't it? He, Akins, hadn't been that far gone, not then. Not yet. Bird-dog a man and at the last, let him slip through your fingers! And the money, too, of course.

The kid wasn't at Guise House, he was nowhere. Nowhere was where Chagro Brannigan was, too. The Seminole was gone, Dutch Gault was gone, the Irishman and the kid vanished like smoke. Again Akins racked his brain. The last train went through here two days ago, a little better than two days ago, it was now. Horses traveled faster than a mule outfit and it would be no problem to catch up.

To all Akins's questions, there were only bright smiles, shrugs, and the spreading of hands. He was wished Godspeed and to come back soon but given no information at all. Chagro's, Sean's, the Indian's, and Dutch Gault's horses were absent from the stable. Akins got his own mount and slammed out of town.

Three nights and two days out of Camargas, the mule string moved through broken, rocky country toward even more tumbled and jagged hills far to the north and east. Beyond these serrated ridges lay the mesas that were the destination of the train. These mesas were all of two miles wide, possibly three miles long, and lush with grass from the spring that rose at the mesas' head and flowed down its center. All around the four sides of this great tableland, the mountains rose to form a gentle cup, but branching off to one side of those mountains was a gap that extended for a good ten miles north toward the lower regions of Texas. From the desert floor, there were no visible openings to this gap, but to someone who knew and who was in a hurry, there was one that could, if followed, cut off a good many miles and offer a measure of protection as well. Another night and day and Chagro and his group would drop off, to lose themselves in the desert and ultimately arrive at the foothills, until it was judged safe to make a run for the border.

Water at the moment was still many miles away, but none of the twenty-six animals was suffering yet. It was unusually hot even for the season, the time just before the rains broke. For days, thunderheads had risen in the east to give a threat of downpour, but there was no rain. Broken by dry winds, the dull gray formations shredded to cotton puffs of white, then settled upon the ridges to dissipate, leaving only a merciless sun blazing from the great, downturned bowl of sky.

It was midafternoon and a surly Dutch, riding flank, again pushed abreast of Chagro. "Can't we shove these bastards along any faster? If we're goin' to get through that notch afore dark, we got to get some speed out of 'em. No damn sense they draggin' their tails like this. I don't like the feel of it—I don't aim to camp out in the open again either, like we done last night. Maybe we better

136

split up with the stuff an' go our separate ways."

Chagro didn't turn; his narrowed eyes searched the skyline. "Sixth time you've sung that same tune in as many miles," he said, "and it's getting to be one big pain in the rear. We can't push 'em any faster, they're going their limit now. We been making good time. Want to kill 'em? If so, we won't get there at all. As for the cut, I should of let you have it back there where you first squawked and you could have done what you damned well pleased with it. Don't keep houndin' me or we'll square up here and now and you can leave—if you figure it's safe to travel alone."

"Maybe I don't want to wait till we come up to the Seminole," Dutch Gault snarled. "That was your idea, not mine. Why wouldn't it be all right to travel alone?"

"Keep your eyes peeled to the hills and you'll soon find out," Chagro retorted. "There's been a half-dozen Indians following us for the last three miles."

"Why don't they attack, then?"

"How in hell do I know why they don't attack? Maybe waitin' for reinforcements. Compared to that bunch, this is a pretty fair-sized outfit, so far. Why should they want to risk their necks?" Keep your gun handy, your eyes sharp, and your flapping mouth shut, Chagro wanted to say. A mile out he'd sighted a following, but that faded when the Indians appeared on the scene. God knew where the rest of the band was and there were sure to be more. The train was coming up to a dry wash and no cover at all, unless you could call cholla and saguaro and thin wisps of sage and creosote bush any kind of protection.

But the mules were holding up well, and the drovers—there were six of them, seven with Carlos, all cheerful. They had been over this route so many times, they could do it with their eyes closed.

The Seminole was somewhere up ahead, they'd cut sign early this morning and followed it until it hit a rocky arroyo, converging there to make some kind of a stand. The men escaped, Chagro was sure, but two mules had fallen and been butchered on the spot and the pieces carried away. Indians could do that. Comanches, Caddo-Comanches, Apaches, or even Utes, the latter two intermarrying from tribe to tribe, occasionally ranged this far south. The Uta and Caddo and, in particular, the Apache bore well-earned reputations, but for sheer viciousness the Comanches in this part of the country outstripped them all. Chagro had seen Mexicans blanch at the name.

He dropped to the rear and scanned the back trail. Akins, too, was out there somewhere. No sign of him yet but there would be. Despite his worry, Chagro had to chuckle at the thought, envisioning the deputy's chagrin at the sneak out. Akins, hamstrung, still could be troublesome and Chagro knew it, for he had never underestimated the man. It could only be hoped that Akins hadn't yet started out, though there was little likelihood of that. After all, there was a limit to what mescal could do, even loaded.

To complicate matters even further, there were

roving bandits with an eye to anything that moved that could be stolen, sold, eaten, or traded, and it was Chagro's notion that the group at Camargas had laid up somewhere to wait for the train to pull out. But the redskins were still the most imminent threat, for that slight puff of dust was reasserting itself on the horizon northward. Where there was one Indian, there could be others, for they moved like shadows at one with the earth, barely discernible to the unwary eye.

At the back of the line, the Mexican, Carlos, raised a hand and pointed. Chagro nodded.

Sean looked around, his face tight. "Pa—?"

"Yeah?"

"There's two of 'em now. One ahead and one behind."

"Yeah." Chagro tried to keep the concern out of his voice and failed. What the hell. The kid was trailwise, he knew already. Fine mess he'd led the boy into. Chagro wanted to say this and more but there wasn't time. "Whatever happens, you do exactly like I tell you. Don't go off half-cocked on some notion of your own, hear?" Then Chagro swung, frowning. That back bunch—didn't look to be many—but was it redskins after all? It was pulling away. What was the reason for that?

"We could give 'em the money," Sean said, "that might stall 'em for awhile. Scatter it around, I mean."

"If it's Indians, what's money to them? They'd want the stock."

Sean shaded his eyes and studied the distance. "You don't think it's Indians?"

"I don't know. Too far away to tell. But I've a hunch it's not—" A rifleshot, far and away on the wind, bespoke its urgent message. Akins? Another shot, and another, and another. Three now, there were three. It was Dan, sure as hell it was Dan, caught in the middle of something.

Chagro straightened sharply, then looked around. "We're going back," he said.

# TWELVE

Akins had seen them coming. Six sly, wiry, little thugs suddenly closed in on him to cut him off, the same run-down Mexican outfit that had tied up in Camargas waiting for a chance to jump something worthwhile. Obviously he was meant to be the key to that something worthwhile, because Brannigan's outfit was too big to tackle. Hostage? Akins thought so. They'd got wind of the gold and meant to force it out of Brannigan that way—it was the gold they wanted.

With overwhelming odds in their favor, the battle should have been brief, except that he'd dropped two of them in that first skirmish, then managed to reach a breastworks of rock, and holed in. It was only temporary shelter at best until they worked around to either side of him, but they had respect for his rifle.

The rock was blistering hot and he could feel sweat seep down under his hatband, the salt perspiration stinging when it reached his eyes.

The horse was dead, gone down with that first challenge. A good horse it was, too, one of the best he'd ever had. Akins regretted that horse.

The stock of the rifle burned against his cheek, and he shifted slightly but keeping the muzzle trained through the notch. Two of them were behind the rocks down below, a third a few yards away off to the left in a thicket of paloverde. He couldn't locate the fourth and it was that one that worried him.

Akins turned his head, again considering his position. There was no way out, no way at all. He was pinned down, and good. There was the smell of dry earth and the scorching heat of the rocks beneath him, and down there were a gathering of little, brown bandits with a plan in their heads. They had it all figured out.

Dan Akins's lips twisted in a wry grin. On ahead somewhere, probably too far away to hear the rifle-shots, would be Chagro. If Brannigan had heard, he'd be wondering.

But for a man pinned down, there wasn't much time to speculate. They hadn't wanted him dead, yet even that was small comfort. The shot that killed his horse had missed its rider by inches as the animal reared; Akins had flung himself from the saddle to hit the ground at a run, bullets kicking up puffs of dust behind him as he reached the rocks and plunged into them. If the intent was to wound and cripple in order to make the capture easier, they had nearly succeeded.

A movement showed in the thinner section of paloverde and Akins squeezed off a shot. There was sharp movement, then silence; a sudden blast of gunfire from below chipped slivers from the boulder nearest his head and the bullet whined off into space. That was close, too close. Akins wiped the blood from his cheek where one of those slivers, sharp as the cutting edge of a knife, had carved a track.

"Come on, you bandy-legged sons of perdition," Akins breathed, and then he heard it. Gunfire—massed—a volley of gunfire, and shouting, sounded in the distance, Brannigan's roar rising above all. Sweeping in, they swiftly surrounded the attackers. Akins scrambled up and came down over the rocks, gun blazing. One wispy character went down, a second rolled, came up to an elbow to send a quick shot and Akins stumbled and fell, clutching his thigh. The neat *spang!* of a rifle put an end to the argument and Sean murmured almost in apology, "I don't like to kill folks but I guess I got to, sometimes. You hurt bad, Mr. Akins?"

Chagro swung from his horse and knelt beside Dan Akins. "Sho—" he chuckled, "just gouged out a chunk, that's all. You're losin' a barrel of blood, though. Let's pack you into some shade and get that bound up. You'll be all right. Son, gimme a hand here."

"If I'd known it was you, I'd have led the parade," Akins said ruefully, and grimaced.

"Last man down's the best," Chagro observed, "what you bellyachin' about? I'm here, ain't I? Don't ask questions."

"You didn't have to come back after me," Akins

growled, "only I'm glad you did. Pulled me out of a hole but I'm sure slowin' down the proceedings. You got an answer for that, too?"

"Dry up," Chagro advised tersely.

Gault, in a brutal mood, fiddled on the sidelines. He kept eyeing the mules. As usual, they were all neatly packed and he hadn't known from the beginning which of them carried the gold. Each night the loads were removed and the animals picketed to graze, and short of rifling those packs, it was still not possible to tell. But there were two, Dutch thought, he was pretty sure there would be two to divide up the load. Gold was heavy, and Brannigan would have given instructions to do it in just the right way—his way. All on his own and without consulting anybody else, of course, Brannigan was good at that. Had to run things, all the way through. And this Akins now, a deputy. What was Brannigan up to, anyway, some kind of a double cross? Gault looked back at Akins and what he thought was plain on his face. He, Gault, could have sent that bullet himself and wouldn't have missed. It would have put a period to Deputy Dan Akins's career once and for all.

"You got any more bright suggestions?" he said to Chagro. "Look at the time we lost. Never will make it up, an' all on account of him."

"Who asked you?" Akins said tightly and accepted a hoist up to saddle. He rode one of the drover's horses, the man walking beside the animal to lead him, and the group swung into line.

An hour they traveled and the heat mounted and

rose from the rocks and earth like a living thing. The air was stifling and the smell of sweat from the horses and mules was rank in their nostrils. Akins swayed, then righted himself with an effort.

"Think you can make it?" Chagro asked.

"Sure. I'll make it. Go on."

Chagro looked at him sharply, noting the deputy's deeply flushed face. Another hour at most, that was about the limit. Chagro rode to the front of the line and spoke briefly to Carlos, the head drover, who nodded. Chagro then returned to position. At the end of the second hour of traveling but still some time short of sundown, Carlos held up a hand, halting the train. "We lay over here."

Gault opened his mouth, observed Chagro's expression, and closed it again. "I owe him one," Brannigan said softly. "It's good for a man to pay his debts, if you got to have a reason. That's all you have to know."

A watch was posted, a fire again kindled, and jerky boiled up to make a nourishing broth, of which Akins drank a little. His leg was swollen but there appeared to be no fever resulting from it; Chagro had cleaned the wound, now dressed it again, and made Akins as comfortable as he could.

Dusk fell swiftly, Sean came over with coffee and handed it to his father. "Be careful," he said. "It's real hot. He's all right, Pa?"

"Oh, sure. Just takes a little watching, is all. I'll sit with him for awhile, you get some sleep."

"I'll sit if you want me to. I ain't sleepy."

"No, not necessary. I told you. All right?"

But the boy still lingered. He stood up, looked

145

around, then sat down again. "Pa, that fire. Can see it clean from here to Texas."

Chagro nodded. "But that was daylight an' we had to have it. Comin' dark now, so set another can of water on in case we need it. After that, bank up the coals all around, then cover 'em with dirt all the way to the sides of the can. That way no fire will show unless you're looking straight down on it. I learned that stunt from a Ute warrior a long time ago—I did him a service. Do it like that, the heat'll hold in but the fire die out by itself. Never any use attractin' any more attention than necessary. If Dan's all right, we'll cut out before daybreak. That's only about four hours from now, so you better roll in. It will be a long, hard grind tomorrow."

"You set a heap of store by folks you like, don't you, Pa? And I guess you like about ever'body."

Chagro didn't answer. The boy cocked his head. "That's a turkey-gobbler? I didn't know turkeys gobbled at night."

"Some do, never heard any around here though."

"And that ain't one?"

"No. Redskins are out there." Carlos, rolled up nearby, had heard it, too. He came to his feet with his gun at the ready. But there was no further sound; Carlos looked over and shrugged.

"Two or three maybe," he said in Spanish. "They make sure how many we are. Now they have seen they go away, I think, not bother us." He lay down again and was almost at once asleep.

"More coffee, Pa?"

"No. You go on."

Sean had one more question. "We going to drop off when we come up with the Seminole?"

"That's the plan."

The boy faded. Dan Akins turned restlessly in his sleep, the mules moved in the darkness, the guards paced. The small fire slowly died and the water can steamed in its nest of coals and dirt.

Chagro sat feeling the night, his thoughts forged far ahead. Deeply disturbed, he turned many things over in his mind. One was the possibility of Dan's wound going bad. There was not much chance of that, but Chagro had seen it happen, with disastrous results. The bullet in this case had laid a long track in the fleshy part of the thigh but not deep enough to touch the bone. It was painful and would be sore for awhile but with luck, shouldn't give any more trouble.

A second factor carried no margin of luck at all; the certainty that the redskins would join forces for a mass attack and it would be a big bunch. That, and the attack itself, were as sure as tomorrow. Nor had the initial flurry by any means ended the threat of bandits, though these tough, little highwaymen usually traveled in smaller groups. But to the redskin, the mule was all important; it meant food, transportation, and to the Comanche, in particular, bargaining power. Comanches had been known to follow a train for scores of miles, waiting until it was in exactly the proper position for its complete annihilation, with no loss to themselves. They had all the time in the world and could afford to wait. Without transportation, food, and water, especially water,

147

anyone escaping such a raid had little chance of survival, for the desert dealt swiftly with its wanderers. Once into the hills, there was shelter in plenty, but they had stopped for Akins, and every hour spent in open country rendered the danger more acute. This Chagro knew, and the Indians were not fools; and thus added one more prediction—there would be big trouble long before the hills were reached.

Akins stirred and woke. "My mouth is mighty dry. I must have ate a bale of cotton. Chagro—that you?"

"How do you feel?"

"Leg hurts like hell, a little lightheaded, otherwise all right. Any water around?" Chagro rummaged for a canteen and Akins hoisted to sitting position, grunting. Daylight was at least two hours off with shadows still dense in the thickets. The drovers, accustomed to early travel, were already stirring.

By noon, they were sixty miles to the east, when a dust cloud wisped up from the rear. Sean climbed to a vantage point to see better. "Soldiers," he reported, "coming fast. A whole lot of 'em. Pa, what'll we do?"

"Can't outrun 'em." Chagro spoke in swift Spanish. "They are not after you, *amigos*, it is only me they want, as you know." He looked around swiftly, glanced at Akins. The deputy's face revealed none of his thoughts. The star caught the bright sunlight and glistened on his chest.

"*Senor*, we could—"

"Forget it. I got you into this, my fault. But they

won't touch you, I'd bank on it. Let it go as it looks."

"Pa—" Sean began, and glanced about wildly.

"No!" Brannigan swore. "And stay back out of the way, no matter what happens, I don't want you in it. Now you mind me!"

"We're not going to do anything—we just going to give up?" The kid's expression was one of anguish, his eyes screwed up and his hands trembled on the rifle.

Chagro grunted and turned away, kicking his horse into motion and the group moved forward. Akins dropped behind and followed more slowly.

Sean whirled, "Mr. Akins, can't you do something? Please, Mr. Akins!"

"Just hold your teeth in your mouth," Akins suggested, "and do like your Pa says. *Exactly* like he says."

"But—"

"Just hold your teeth in your mouth," Akins repeated, "an' act like nothing's wrong."

Gault, who had been riding point, galloped back. "We're in a fix—I could swear them're soldiers back there! What we goin' to do?"

"You're going to get lost," Akins snapped,"—quick! This bunch is rollin' too close together an' raisin' too much dust for 'em to figure out just one man. Hunt yourself a hole an' crawl into it an' send back your horse. Get it? Send back your horse! Damn it, make tracks if you want to save your skin!"

Dutch Gault awaited no further explanation, he melted into a paloverde thicket and presently his horse emerged riderless; Carlos mounted and they proceeded as before.

The pursuers were coming up fast. "Chagro," Akins called, "catch," and a pair of handcuffs sailed through the air. "Snap these on."

"What the hell—!"

"Better move on it," Akins barked, and Brannigan did as he was told.

# THIRTEEN

There were twenty in the bunch, eighteen military and two women, Pilar and Annabelle Weems. Akins barely suppressed his shock at the sight. Brannigan scowled, his face like a thundercloud. Akins noticed the scowl and glanced away, because he knew what Chagro was thinking.

"Who is in charge here?" A slim, aristocratic lieutenant pushed forward.

"I am." Akins held up a hand, then identified himself, to which the lieutenant nodded briefly, his black eyes roving the outfit in a businesslike way. Carlos he knew, he dismissed Carlos, the other drovers.

The soldier's head jerked to Sean. "Who is he?"

Chagro spoke up. "Son. He goes where I go, see?"

"And you are *Senor* Brannigan," the officer purred, "unless I am very much mistaken. I have heard of you—not all good, I fear." He turned again to Akins. "We have also heard . . . other things. We demand to search those packs."

Akins hawked, spat, shook his head. "Not while I'm in charge, you don't." He spoke grimly. "I'm an officer of the law transportin' my prisoner to the border. I've searched those bags and there's nothin' in 'em. We're stringin' along with this outfit for protection—Injuns an' bandits lousy in this area. You should know."

The lieutenant stiffened. "There are bandits everywhere, *Senor!* And I hardly think your explanation is sufficient to—"

"Pull up a chair an' sit down," Chagro invited sarcastically. "Sure you wouldn't want us to serve drinks? Party's gettin' thick. Sorry we can't offer high-class entertainment. Maybe on the other hand—" he indicated the cuffs. "Stick around, there might be."

It was a ticklish moment, for that moment decision hung in the balance. Akins tipped it. "Anything further I can do for you gentlemen?" he wanted to know. "If not, I think I'll move around a bit to keep the stiffness out of my leg. Some of your *compadres* jumped us awhile back an' one of 'em left his callin' card. Not bad, but does give me a twinge now an' again." He looked up all at once, his eyes steely. "If you're thinkin' on it, don't, 'less you want to tangle with the United States Gov'ment, who might be more than willin' to tangle. This man has voluntary give himself up an' what he does from here on in is my responsibility. As for what you heard, I've never seen none of it. You got my word on that."

The officer hesitated. There was truth to what

the lawman said and he knew it, moreover, he himself had little actual authority in the matter. For some time, relations had been strained between his own government and that of the United States, but they had greatly improved and the orders were that in no way must ill feeling be engendered to disrupt those relations. It was entirely possible that nothing would be gained and much forfeited by tampering with *Norteamericano* law, even to the loss of his own commission. The lieutenant shuddered to think. Still—

"There were two other men, were there not? Where are they?"

"Count us," Akins invited. "I'm not custodian of the whole country, just him. After a merry chase, I'm happy enough."

"Very well. I suppose I must agree, though— Very well! However, you could have been more cooperative. I shall report it to my commanding officer—"

"Do that," Akins agreed dryly.

The lieutenant swung his horse, rapping out an order and the troop fell into line. There was a stir in the ranks and Pilar's voice rose strongly against it. "I gave no reason. I needed no reason! You as military were traveling where I wished and obliged to take me, a civilian, when I request. Of course, I am not going back!"

"Nor I," piped Annabelle Weems.

Pilar pulled her horse aside to line up with the mule train. "I have accept' your so gallant escort and that of your men," she stated, "but now it is finished. I thank you and goodbye, Lieutenant."

The officer was clearly shocked. "And you," he demanded, facing Annabelle Weems, "why did you come?"

"To find my husband," Annabelle said demurely. "*I* have nothing to hide. I am most anxious to see him—you understand. It has been so long! You may not be aware of it, sir, but once before I made a determined effort to reach the United States but was driven back by Indians. I knew when Mr. Akins left the village that he would be heading for the border and that he would not refuse me escort. He knows my husband and how anxious I am that we be reunited. There is no one better qualified to carry a mission through to a conclusion, nor one who would provide a more safe escort. I trust Mr. Akins implicitly. So you see, Lieutenant, I am in good hands, and you may set your mind at rest. And I do thank you." Annabelle smiled prettily, the officer could only accept the edict.

The party swept away in the direction it had come. Pilar tried to catch Chagro's eye and failed; he made a sharp gesture with his hand and she fell back.

Akins rode up beside Chagro. "Well, they're gone. How are international relations, anyway? Hope I didn't stick my foot in too deep."

"You said right," Chagro said briefly. "It was what changed his mind."

Akins wiped off a grin. "I see your women followed you. Missin' one though, or maybe a lot of 'em I don't know about."

"You think it's funny. What in hell am I supposed to do with two women? Somethin' else— you mean me to wear these things from now on or do I get out of them?" Brannigan indicated the cuffs.

Akins produced the keys, unlocked the handcuffs, and restored both key and cuffs to his pocket. A glance back over his shoulder showed the two girls riding far apart, one on one side of the train, the other on the opposite side. Akins grunted. "You catch that line of bull the Weems woman was handin' out? What's her real purpose, anyway?"

Brannigan rubbed his wrists. "To make trouble. She's a born troublemaker. I thought I was rid of her."

"And me?" Akins suggested.

"When we come to the fork in the road, they go with you," Brannigan said. "My thanks for what you did but from now on, we're even."

"The hell we are! We'll never be even, you an' me. Ain't you tumbled to that yet?" Akins's eyes sought Brannigan's tight face, his own look serious and speculative. "I know how you feel. What can I say? You can still chuck the business an' come on with me. I know you didn't do those murders. You got the money but a lifetime of worry's not worth it. Tell Dutch you're throwin' it over and face him down. Then of the three that leaves only the Seminole. I don't know him too well but you do and you can maybe figure out what he'd think. Return the money and the case is half won. You got Sean now, most of all in this

155

you got to think of him."

Brannigan's narrowed gaze rested on the bright, glaring distance, the atmosphere so hot it seemed to vibrate. "See that lake?" He gestured. Southward on the flat desert floor a mirage shimmered, clear and beautiful. The water almost appeared to ripple in the sun, the illusion was so complete. "Real pretty blue. Got edges of sand an' everything. You can see it sparkle. Makes a man, all sweaty and layered with ground-in dirt, feel like he'd give about all he had to jump right in. Skin can almost feel it, taste it. You paint a pretty picture, Dan, but it's no more true than that lake. If I'd fired those shots, I'd expect to be hung but damned if I'll go down for somethin' I didn't do because I can't prove it, even for a kid like Sean. Especially for a kid like Sean. He needs a Dad, even one like me. I can finish raisin' him one jump ahead of the law as well as any other way."

"I stood behind you this time, didn't I?"

Brannigan rubbed the stubble on his big jaw and nodded. "Yeah, you did. But this is different."

"Trust me."

"No, an' I don't want to talk about it anymore. I got things to do an' I better keep my mind on 'em. That something up ahead—other than a mirage, I mean?"

Dutch, having rejoined the train and claimed his horse, was prodding an argument with one of the drovers. Chagro rode forward. "Lay off," he suggested. "These fellows are doing you a service or maybe you don't know it. It's because of them we're getting where we're going, and in force, but we're only carrion drawin' the flies. They didn't have to have us along—we're just extra baggage, us an' our cargo."

"When you goin' to let go of some of that cargo?"

Chagro hesitated, then came to a decision. "We should catch up with the Seminole sometime tomorrow. We'll divide it then."

Dutch showed his broken teeth in a grin. "By God," he exulted, "by God—! Ten thousand! What can't a man do with ten thousand? All the money in the world. I'm goin' to buy me a ocean of booze an' a houseful of women an' wallow in 'em the rest of my life." He paused, then looked at Chagro suspiciously. "What you givin' it to me tomorrow for?"

"Because you asked," Chagro retorted, "and I'm sick of hearin' you spill your guts every time we turn around. There's other things in the world more important than money, like stayin' alive. High time you took some of the responsibility yourself."

"Once I get my share, I don't have to hang around."

"No, you don't. But we need your guns, you need ours. The only way we'll get through is by stickin' together. You know as well as I do what's waitin' out there, or should. If you want to play patty cake alone against a pack of blood-hungry savages, go ahead. It's your choice."

"What about the women?"

Chagro jerked around, startled. "What about 'em?"

Gault leered. "One's a looker—the Mex gal, an' out here it's every man for himself. She's real somethin'. The other—"

"Tackle Pilar she'll rip your liver out. The other's Jeff Weems's wife. Tackle her *he'll* rip your liver out. Better knock that notion before it hatches."

Sean came riding back. "Crossed deer track up ahead, Pa. Not usual for deer to be roamin' this far down, is it?"

"Sometimes they do." He grinned at the boy, tremendously cheered. Whatever happened, he had the kid, they had each other. They'd make it out of this somehow, they had to. "It's meat for the pot so get him if you can," he instructed, "but don't go too far out."

Chagro dropped to the rear for the first opportunity he'd taken to talk to Pilar. He was still angry.

"I am sorry," she said in a small voice without looking at him.

"You're sorry," he stated bitterly. "That explains everything. You knew what you were getting into. What's in those packs and what I've done makes me an outlaw, and now you're right along with me."

"I know. I remembered all that. And I know what you are thinking, about how useless I am. But I can shoot as good as any man. I can be a help, not a hindrance. I will not get in your way—I never get in your way. You will see."

"Yeah? This is no Sunday-school picnic like you seem to think. It puts me in a hell of a fix, having you along—and her. I told you I'd come back. What made you pull a stunt like this anyway?"

"I am sorry," Pilar murmured again. Her shoulders drooped; she added simply, "There was nothing left for me in Camargas with you gone." Annabelle looked on jealously. "I should feed her to the wolves, maybe," Pilar said with a vicious sidewise glance. "Maybe her husband come soon."

"Sure," retorted Chagro. "That's all we need. The more, the merrier. That business about bein' able to fight—you might have to. Keep it in mind."

Sean rode up ahead, his gaze going ceaselessly back and forth under the brim of his battered hat. There were no more tracks of deer and the animal seemed to have vanished. Behind him twenty-six mules plodded, the small hooves kicking up puffs of dust that rose in a cloud to settle like a dun, gray blanket on man and beast.

He turned in the saddle and looked back. Drovers and flankers, his father, all of them rode as vague and shifting shadows within that cloud. He heard the Weems woman's sharp voice flung out in mockery and the Mexican girl's grated reply, "No!"

For a long time, he had resented the money in his father's keeping. It was, he thought, the cause of all their trouble. That and Dutch Gault. The Seminole he liked, and he liked the girl, Pilar, though she spoke seldom to him and never exhibited any reaction other than impatience when he was around. Still, she would get used to him and he sensed her warmth underneath, but because of the uneasy situation that existed between her and his father, was afraid to show it. She was no barwoman either, hers was one of the oldest families in Mexico, once the owners of vast acres, the family decimated by accident, by bandits and Indians, so now only she remained. He had seen her laugh, seen her smile, and most of all, how her eyes lit up for his father. Together they would make a home, she would be a good step-mother, for that was what would happen if they got out of this.

They were entering more broken country, the flatland giving way to pockets of sand and sage where only barren earth had existed before, and frequent arroyos, sharply cut by seasonal rains, showed bleached-white rocks in their depths. Here swift waters had run and would run again in the thunderstorms; men and animals often were swept away in treacherous flash floods where water pouring down those gullies increased in depth from an inch or two to several feet in a matter of minutes. But this would not happen today or tomorrow, for he liked to notice those things. Last night's sunset had glowed blood-red, and still no cloud or hint of cloud marred the horizon.

Under the hot afternoon sky, the mountains were crumpled gold, dotted here and there with darker clumps of brush. Nearer in, the foothills showed gray-green from sage and mesquite, with a sprinkling of oak in the ravines.

The third and fifth mules carried those sacks

and Sean could see them clearly in his mind: canvas, they were, with leather straps. Many a sack was made that way but these had ingenious closures, with a leather thong folding over to form a loop at the top for easy lifting and carrying. These mule men should be paid and that was all right, but he'd heard his father say Dutch was to get his share tomorrow. Then the Seminole, for his father had a loyalty and would not let these people down. It was like giving his word and he would not break it now. So the gold would be scattered to the four winds. Scattered—

A desert hare suddenly bolted across in front of him and Sean alerted. The rifle, carried always in the crook of his arm, swung at once. It was then he noticed the rock beside the trail. He stared at that rock. Abruptly he lifted the gun and fired, and the rock became a blanketed Indian, whirling up and away, then collapsing on the earth.

Chagro shouted and spurred forward, and the train came to a halt, bunching together. Other riders hurried up, Chagro knelt to make his brief examination. "Comanche, on a little scouting foray." He nodded to Sean. "Quick eyes. We need quick eyes in this business. You may have saved a mule from bein' hamstrung, or a knife in somebody's chest." Chagro rose and looked around; he and Carlos exchanged glances. Carlos nodded slowly. "There's more of his little brown brothers in the hills," Chagro said, "or maybe not that far away. Funny they haven't hit us before. Must be busy doin' somethin' else. I'd like to know what."

"Where there's one, there could be more," Akins

observed. "We better double the guard tonight."

In the background, Annabelle Weems had lifted her voice in a shriek, then settled down to weeping noisily.

Carlos came close to Brannigan. "You feel something?" he asked.

"Trouble," Brannigan said, "it's all around us out there, like fog."

# FOURTEEN

It was late afternoon of the second day after leaving the Pozo Ahumada, and true to the agreement, Dutch had his gold. Nothing would induce him to remain, so he rode out, headed by his own reckoning to the border. Akins had looked on grimly but remained silent through all this, knowing how little good it would do to protest or to try to put a stop to it. The Seminole would wait to claim his share, he said, it was safe enough where it was. Yes, he had seen Indians, there was a skirmish, but it was a small band and had been driven off.

"The train I was with went on to the mesas," he said. "With my two packhorses, one with the bell—" here he smiled slightly, "and myself, we made out fine. There are very good caves at the base of the cliffs."

"I know them well," Carlos agreed," I myself have hidden there when the need arose."

Akins had stepped aside and was examining the

bell. It was old, not very large as bells went, not as big as some he had seen, fashioned of bronze corroded green, with the ring holding the clapper bent, but it had a proud flare and the gift would make the villagers of little Isleta very happy.

The Seminole had looked at Akins sharply at first, then appeared to accept the deputy's presence, satisfied to leave it up to Brannigan.

Brannigan was worried, Dan could tell that. It showed in his restless urgency, his quick alertness to sound and motion, the way he kept glancing over his shoulder. They were riding too openly, he, the Seminole, and the kid, with Pilar trailing along cheerful and disconsolate by turns.

Ahead, the shoulder of Agua Bacia loomed black against the sky, and here was water, but Bacia was still more than twenty miles away. Water was scant in all the holes, for it had been an unusually dry spring, and though it was now late July, there was still no rain. The Pozo, like many wells in this section of Mexico, was nearly dry; they were forced to dig through a crust of dried mud and wait for moisture to seep in. It had taken hours to water the mules, fill the canteens and the emergency kegs.

Travel was now at night to take advantage of the coolness and thus conserve both water and energy, for the mules were beginning to show the strain of the long hard drive.

This trail to the mesas was the one most commonly used and lay fairly straight as the crow flies. Carlos and his men had followed the route for years, taking advantage of the known tinajas and seeps, but the weather was playing them false. All agreed that when the rain came, it would be a good one.

They drove on, setting a course by the stars but ever watchful, for the night had a thousand ears and eyes, and near dawn they drew up to rest the mules and to camp. Wind soughed lightly along the ground, and far out on the plateau a coyote cried. Sean left the fire and cocked his head to listen. Turning, he found his father beside him.

"Pa, it's got so I make something out of everything I hear. Danger, I mean, even a simple, little, old animal. But that don't sound quite like a animal. I can't explain it but it's just a mite different. I make out that's no coyote—or am I just bein' uneasy?"

"No, you're not," and Chagro said again, "they're out there," knowing the Indians had been following all along.

"What do you s'pose they're up to?"

Chagro grunted. "Hard to guess. Some notion of their own. God only knows."

"Pa, I've kind of had the idea you're of pity for the Indians. You got a feelin' for them, too?"

"Like anything stepped on," Brannigan admitted, "like you'd be for a thing stepped on. But that doesn't mean," he added grimly, "that I'd let 'em tramp on me. If it's got to be me or them, it's no choice. Man doesn't walk up to redskin an' give him that advantage."

"Think they got Dutch?"

The question was unexpected and Chagro hesitated. "I don't know," he said.

As soon as the train stopped, Annabelle had immediately sunk to the ground, so dead beat there was no fight left in her. Pilar, on the other hand, moved purposefully about gathering fuel for a fire. Akins presently came over and lifted the sticks from her arms, insisting that she rest, and she thanked him gratefully.

Preparing to walk away, he swung at her call. "Mr. Akins, is there—is there anything I can do? I mean, I have not been much help so far. Sometimes I think I should not have come, and it will always be this way, that I am not wanted."

"He's just mad. Give him time."

She shook her head sadly. "I think it is more than that. I have gone too far and it is not the same. He has not looked at me or talked to me for a long time. What am I to do? If it was not so far I would—"

"Go back?"

"No," she said. When Akins looked again, he found her smiling; her shoulders were straight, her chin held high.

He grinned and touched his hat. "Good girl," he said.

"Mr. Akins, you have a wife?"

"And a little boy, yes."

"Then you understand. This is not for just a little while. It is worth waiting for. I talk much but, except for sometimes, it is only talk."

Later he carried coffee to them both, gravely hearing out Annabelle's tale of woe. The two women were still not speaking, nor, he knew, would they. They were worlds apart and would remain that way, but as long as they kept out of each other's hair, so much the better. Silence—he looked at Annabelle again—was golden. Akins rejoined the others at the blaze.

But the air of the group was one of unease. Shadows seemed to undulate in the ghostly predawn black, with only the small and ineffectual glow of the fires to shut out an alien and unfriendly world; when a coyote wept again men, raised their heads to listen.

"Damn yappin' ridgerunners," somebody said. "Caused hair to rise on more necks than'd patch hell a mile. Wish he'd shut up. Gives me the creeps."

"It's not like—" somebody else began, and then harked to a long drawn-out scream, inhuman from a human throat, the last drop of guttering life. Men leaped to their feet, Akins with his gun drawn, but Carlos was before him.

"No—do not go out there, *Senor!* It is what they want."

Brannigan's arm was an effective bar across the kid's chest; the boy had his rifle trained into the dark.

"Never mind, never mind. It's over. All done."

"Who was it?" Pilar whispered. She came close and touched Chagro's shoulder. Her eyes were huge but her voice was steady; there was no panic. She was in full possession of herself. "Dutch?" she asked and read her answer in Chagro's set face.

"Get back out of the light an' keep out of the light," he ordered, "just to be on the safe side. But there's no danger now. They've done what they meant to do. Christ!" he swore.

Dawn was pearly light, gently tracing the contours of the land, tree and bush and rock thrust up through the opalescence like miniature ships in an ocean of fog. That light grew and melted the last of the shadows, but there was a dark lump of something left upon the earth that was neither rock nor shrub.

It lay on its back, arms outflung and eyes wide and sightless to the new day, and its throat had been cut from ear to ear. There were many knife wounds upon the body, cleverly placed, for an Indian good at the business knows ways, of which the white man never dreamed, to keep his victim alive as long as he wishes that victim to remain so. The horse and pack were gone, and a canvas sack slit with its contents strewn carelessly upon the ground. The Indians had vanished, the morning was empty and benign.

"So goes a man," the Seminole murmured, "and with him all his bitterness and hate and hope."

Chagro turned away, his big jaws set. "Get the shovels," he said, "we'll bury what's left of him. It's the least we can do."

"Hell of a way to die," Akins growled. He looked sick.

They prepared to move on, Sean was already mounted and out front, and the line formed.

Annabelle had come out of her faint; she held a dusty handkerchief to her nose and peered over it. "You are just going to leave all that money lying there?"

Brannigan looked down at her. He felt he had

never seen the woman before, that he was now seeing her for the first time. "If you want it, pick it up. Go ahead, it's all yours. But if you pick it up, you pack it, God damn it, if you have to wear it around your neck. Gold—I'm gettin' sick of the word, sick of the worry." Then it occurred to him that the bits of yellow metal could represent a lifetime of gain to these faithful men who so quietly and with fatalism looked on. Nor had they yet been paid, so Brannigan gathered what had been dropped.

"Take it, you've earned it."

Carlos drew back. "I want nothing," he said. "It has blood on it, the price of a man, before this is finished, perhaps the price of many men. Now I am free, then I would not be. It is bad luck, not alone this, but all of it is bad luck. Trouble would come after us if we took it." Carlos looked around uneasily. "*Senor* Chagro, I am sorry but that is the way I feel, and so, I think, do these others also."

A murmur of assent swept the group; there was one who hesitated, then shook his head. "I dare not," he said. "Carlos is right. It is cursed."

"You see?" Carlos asked. "This gold," he muttered, "it would perhaps be better if all of it were thrown away."

Loyal, enduring, generous to a fault, the Mestizo, of mixed blood, was often more Indian than Mexican, and heir to all the dark superstitions of his race. Talking wouldn't change their minds.

"Still not fair," Brannigan insisted gruffly. "I'll put it in a saddlebag for you. Dutch won't be spendin' his share where he's gone, anyhow."

"Never seen thirty thousand treated more casual," Akins remarked, "or ten thousand either."

Chagro didn't answer, yet later when the boy asked, Chagro replied, "Who knows why an Injun does what he does? To show his contempt, I reckon." The boy turned, watching his father, watching Akins, head thoughtfully tipped as though listening to an inner voice.

Akins shook Brannigan's shoulder. It was late afternoon and Chagro, despite having stood the last watch, opened his eyes and was instantly awake.

"What's up?"

"Dust on the horizon, coming on our back trail. Might not mean anything an' again it might. Can't tell how many, it's still too far away."

Carlos was already up, the others rising and buckling on their guns. The kid stirred and roused. "Pa, is there trouble?"

"Don't know yet." Chagro sat up and tugged on his boots, then rose and stamped into them. Catching up his rifle, he slipped out to a thicket and beyond it to a scarp of rocks. Not Indians, it wouldn't be Indians. Indians didn't announce themselves that way. You never saw redskins until they rose out of the earth and air and then it was usually too late. Brannigan climbed to the cliff, and from this higher point he had his look and immediately went back to camp.

"There's a little wind," he said to Akins, "but it's stirring up a lot of dust back there. Looks like only one man and I'll lay you ten to one it's Jeff Weems. Couldn't wait and he's coming on ahead."

"Alone? He must want her pretty bad." Akins glanced over his shoulder at Annabelle, gracelessly sprawled and sleeping with her mouth open. "Well," Akins added, "guess this is it, because you'll be lightin' out right quick. Weems didn't come by himself, he'll have his bunch close behind him, which'll be the rest of the posse. I wouldn't give 'em much leeway, either. I'll cover for you," Akins said. "If you're damn fool enough to jump in an' lose your head, it'll be the last thing I can do for you."

Emotion rose thick in Brannigan's throat but he could let none of it out in words. He thrust out a hand, Akins met it in a firm grip.

Brannigan swiftly saddled his horse, Sean and the Seminole following suit, and the packs were quickly lashed on.

"Thirty miles from this place in the direction of Perdidas Mujeres is an ancient mision whose ruins will hide you." Carlos came close and spoke rapidly. He pointed. "Near here in that direction is a butte with a shoulder that will quickly cut you off from view. God go with you."

"And the gold," muttered Akins and swore a round oath. This made him a liar and a cheat, with no honor left in him for the badge he wore. His own wrists might as well have worn the cuffs, his own hands spirited away the gold. What he, Dan Akins, had done and would yet do made him as guilty as they. Could he, he thought again, have made the break for it to salvage the money on his own? Risk was one thing but foolhardiness something else, a traveler alone assured of the same fate as Dutch's. But this—this went against the grain, against all those principles he lived by, acknowledged in their deeper meanings, and what he had sworn to uphold that hot afternoon long ago at the Barrancas when Sheriff Dawson pinned the star on him.

He watched Brannigan melt into the brush with the other two horses and the pack animal following. Akins turned then, searching all around, and in that vast empty space, there was no living thing but a lone buzzard circling watchfully high above. Heat waves shimmered in the distance and there was no movement, no sign of life save the slight tremor of leaves and brush where Chagro and the others had passed through.

Then he saw it, to the west a thin spiral of smoke twisted almost lazily upward to lose itself in the limitless blue of sky, and closer in, to cut off that oncoming group, still another. Twin smokes from twin peaks.

Pilar had stood stiffly to watch Chagro leave, held back only by his terse command. Now she drew her breath in sharply. "Indians?"

"The same."

"We're in for it." Akins shouted the alarm, at the same moment, Sean and the others spurred back.

"You fellows getting company," Sean yelled, "look—!" And Carlos's cry ran down the ranks, "Load up, load up—we must try for better shelter!"

"Indians? Where?" Annabelle cried, now fully awake.

"One jump behind your husband an' may his britches escape the fire, for the salvation of us all," rejoined Akins and he looked up to Chagro's swift grin. "You around again?" he said. "Thought we'd got rid of you for sure. Come on—let's get out of here!"

# FIFTEEN

The mules bunched together and milled, confused and frightened at the sudden uproar. Then hazed by the wild shouts of the men and guns fired into the air, they broke into motion. Chagro spurred beside them yelling, slapping with his coiled rope to tighten up the string, and with his horse nipping at the stragglers.

The direction was due south with Jefferson Weems coming up from the west. A quarter mile beyond Weems, riding like fury, for they had seen the smokes and knew all too well what they meant, were the six remaining men of Sheriff Dawson's old posse.

It was a long way from Camargas, farther yet from Dos Brazos, and the manhunt, begun so long ago, was near an end and the pursued almost within grasp. But they were not thinking of these things now, they were riding for their lives.

All except Weems, who was riding for revenge. Even at this moment, revenge was uppermost in his mind. He meant to face Brannigan down, and with a wronged husband's jealous rage carried and mounted to killing intensity, meant to make him pay for the seduction, the kidnapping, all of it. He, Jefferson Weems, would do this even if he died for it.

The destination of the train was a rise thinly protected on two sides by a semicircle of stony hogback, with a fair view from these two sides and the slope falling below. Not a good spot but better than the one they had just left, and the men set about at once reinforcing it with piled rocks to make a higher protective barrier all around the edges.

This was off their course and exceedingly rough country, with the black butte of Boca Negra rising some four miles distant and Sardis Peaks marking the gateway into deeper Mexico. It was an area cut by numerous canyons and dry ridges, the latter showing sparse outgrowth of ocotillo, sage, and mesquite, with an occasional barrel cactus and now and again a tall suguaro. The spot they had reached was one known only to Carlos in passing, but it afforded some shelter for the stock, this being a narrow basin hemmed in with rocks and having at its opening a huge boulder. In this basin horses and mules would be secure for a time, with access only from above. Here Carlos posted a man to keep watch. Horses were quickly unsaddled, mules unloaded and kegs lifted down and carefully stowed, for there was no water otherwise. Save for what little remained in the canteens, animals and men were now dependent upon the kegs.

Sure of themselves and their objective, the Indians were moving down from the hills at an almost casual pace. Free-flowing, a long, serpentine, brown line, so long Sean stared in disbelief.

"Pa—look."

"All we can handle," stated Akins grimly, and to Chagro and the Seminole nearby, "You should of kept going, see what you got into. Damn shame we had to run away from those fellows comin' up, but what else could we do?"

"That means Weems," Brannigan said, "and look at him come. Really burnin' up the dust. But the others—God, it's hard to sit here and watch men die. Those murderin' red bastards!" The second line of Indians closing up from the opposite direction was smaller, but it was this one that overtook the six to cut off part of it for destruction. It was too far away and there was nothing anybody could do. What happened was inevitable. It was watching a panorama of death but mercifully over very soon.

For the Indians caught the stragglers. Frank Hastings and a man named Bemis were both shot from their horses, and an old wrangler, Owen Cooley, died clawing at an arrow that went through his throat. In falling, his foot caught in the stirrup and Cooley was dragged near to the safety he could no longer appreciate before his mount, mortally wounded, collapsed. Jeff Weems first, then the three others remaining, had hit the enclosure at a dead gallop and rolled from their horses, the following Indians for the moment drawn off and keeping well out of range.

Weems turned over and sat up, scrubbing the

dirt and sweat from his face. There was no preamble. "Brannigan!" he roared. "I want to talk to you!" Annabelle, weeping noisily, had thrown herself upon her husband, but he disengaged her arms and thrust her aside, not gently.

Chagro shifted from his knees. He squatted back on his heels and in an almost leisurely fashion, drew out papers and tobacco and proceeded to build a careful cigarette, as though all his attention was drawn to this one act. He struck a match and applied it, head tipped against the smoke curling up around his face.

"All right," he said. "Talk. I figure we got about ten minutes, so make it fast."

"You got somethin' to say for yourself afore I shoot you down like the yella, wife-stealin' dog you are?" Weems panted. His face was livid and temper, Akins saw, had carried the man away completely. The Seminole, Carlos, and the others watched without speaking, Sean's eyes glittered with outrage. He moved the rifle around so it trained on Weems; Chagro pressed him back and stood up, stretching to full height.

"What's your beef?" Chagro wanted to know, still mild and even. "An' you better state it plain, I'm a simple man myself."

"You seduced my wife, caused her to run away with you. You kidnapped her an' forced her to stay with you."

"I—what?" Chagro thumbed back his hat, his broad face creased in a sudden grin. "Look, I didn't force her to anything. Ask Akins here. You want to know the truth? She followed me out of Brazos—wasn't my idea. Swiped a horse—"

177

"Best horse in my stables!"

"Well, don't blame me for that. The horse knew the way if she didn't, the poor devil was after water. Trail horse, wasn't he? Didn't need no map to tell him where to find it. I figure I've said about enough, you believe what you damn well want to believe for the rest of it."

"Then why'd she leave?" Weems demanded. He was beginning to simmer down a bit, Akins saw this with relief.

"How'd I know?" Chagro cocked an eyebrow at the frightened Annabelle and shrugged. "Lovers' spat, maybe. Don't you know anything about women? She had a mad on an' ran away from you—I was handy, that's all. I couldn't stop her goin' along. You want any more particulars, ask her. I had plans of my own. What do you think—that I had her in one of my saddlebags somewhere? Come to your senses, man! I had no rope on her."

"You mean that she—"

"Hell, I wouldn't wish that on my worst enemy."

"*What—!*"

Brannigan made a move to turn away, there was an ominous click behind him. Chagro whirled lightning fast and there was a gun in his fist. But he was still smiling and pleasant. "Get back out of the way, Pilar," he ordered the girl, and gestured. And to Weems, "You come chargin' in primed for bear. All worked up to a froth an' ready to fight. I got no quarrel with you or anybody else here, but I've had my say and I'll stand by it. I don't want your wife, never did. Is that plain enough? Take

178

her, she's all yours. But if you're of a notion to make something of it otherwise, go ahead. Let's get it over with."

"Why, you—"

Weems was pushing, he was staring death in the face and too stupid to know it. "Hold on!" Akins ordered sharply. "Hold it right there! You got your wife back, Jeff, now we—all of us—got somethin' else facin' us. I suggest we give our attention to that."

But Weems, still stinging, had one further argument. "Then how'd she get here if you didn't bring her along for him, or if he didn't take her?"

Akins told him curtly and sparing none of the details. He had no patience with Annabelle, he knew her too well. If she got back in her husband's good graces, it would be of her own doing, nobody else's. Jeff should know what a little trollop she was and did already, if he had a brain in his head.

The three new men, Darcey, Frobish, and Jarstad, had hunkered down near Akins.

"That all of it?" one of them said. It was Darcey, a hostler's helper from Dos Brazos, a small dark man given to much thought.

"All of what? The argument?" Akins mopped his forehead, gazing at the sky. Three hours of daylight left and clouding up real thick. Maybe it would rain. But what good would that do? The horses and mules were restless too, so closely confined. They were feeling the weather and the unrest in the air. "It damn well better be all of it, if I have to jam a rifle stock down somebody's throat. I'm sick of the yammerin'—let 'im fight with his wife. Man's nerves enough on edge anyway."

"Where's the other one—Gault?"

"Dead. Injuns got him." Darcey nodded but said no more. Jarstad, a heavy, red-necked Swede, appeared puzzled but asked no questions.

Frobish growled at Akins' elbow, "So that's the slippery Brannigan we been trailin' so long, caged at last." He had been eyeing Chagro.

"Caged!" Akins snorted. "It's not him that's caged. He come back to help out."

"Still a outlaw," insisted Frobish. "If he come back like you say he did, he must have give himself up. Surrendered, ain't he? How come you haven't put the manacles on him?"

"Manacles?" Akins snapped. "We're not all of us goin' to come out of this alive, mister, remember that when you expect a man to fight around handcuffs. We need every gun we can get."

The Swede said something to Darcey, to which the latter replied, "No, and he ain't got fiery eyes and a forked tail, either. A man who'd put himself in a bind to scrap for others can't be all bad. I never believed half that stuff I heard anyway. Ask ourselves an hour, two hours from now and see what we think, if anybody's still around."

"Maybe he come back because he had to," mumbled Jarstad. "Them Indians didn't look like pussycats to me."

"Think again, Ole. They had a head start and the Indians was concentratin' on us. A man could have got away. We did. Traveling light and moving fast, he could do it."

But the obdurate Frobish was not to be dissuaded. "Who says he'd be travelin' light. The

180

gold's here, ain't it? Unless he's got it buried in the hills somewhere. Injuns is Injuns to me. Look at that one sittin' over there grinnin', like a cat over a saucer of cream. Bet he could tell us."

Crouched down behind his rock, Sean tightened. He looked over at his father but said nothing.

In the brief lull, Weems's voice rose angrily. "Behave yourself or I'll bash you silly. Hear? I'm of no mind to dally with hot-butt, runnin'-off wimmen. When we get home, I'll make up my mind what to do with you. I may keep you, I may not. Depends on how I feel."

"Jefferson—"

"Shut *up!*" Annabelle subsided.

Akins suddenly raised an arm. "Here they come boys, here—they—come!"

The cry was taken up by other throats, Carlos's *"Vienen, hombres, vienen!"* risen sharply.

They came with a rush, spreading out, whooping, confident of swift victory in that first crushing onslaught. But the defense inside the enclosure was keen, with each man tightened down grimly to his job, choosing his target and squeezing off, watching an attacker fall or his horse go down.

An Indian hurled himself from his mount, lit running, and with great strides, darting and dodging, managed to gain the rocks below; when he crouched for another spurt, Brannigan laid his shot where the Indian's chest should be, and was. The warrior threw up his arms and pitched to the ground. Another, slid down behind his pony's neck, slipped past to fire pointblank at Akins, the bullet narrowly missing its target.

"Close," Akins grunted. "Man, that one had my name on it, I swear. Somebody up there must be watchin' over me."

Sean centered his rifle carefully and caught an oncoming Comanche in midstride. The man seemed to pause, like a great grotesque bird, then collapsed.

"How do you feel about killing now?" Chagro asked.

"I still don't like it."

"Well, don't get to like it. I'm countin' on that. It's no job for a man unless he's got to do it." The two exchanged brief glances and the boy's smile was thin and white, but steady. "I'll make out. Pa, you be careful."

"Sure." From the corner of his eye, Brannigan caught a stir in the mesquite off to his right; he fired and instantly two bullets cut sharply across the sound of a third, all three smashing into the rock below his face. They were getting the range now and had found the openings between the boulders.

All around there was heavy firing. Weems in his nervous excitement threw lead too wildly to accomplish much, but the three new men were doing their part. Darcey was kneeled down shooting steadily, Frobish's heavier weapon overriding it with a full-throated roar, and Jarstad's '44 steadily tipped shots into the melee. All three were experienced and had fought Indians before, Darcey with wagon trains, Frobish as a trapper among the Blackfeet in '41, Jarstad who, when only a boy had seen his family massacred by the Sioux, and had grown up fighting Indians. All were solid Dos

Brazos citizens, good and responsible men, embarked upon a manhunt with every belief in its justness, every determination to pursue it to its grim conclusion. And here, Jarstad thought, was their quarry, the hunted one, thief and killer of two innocent persons, joined in wholeheartedly against a common enemy. He hadn't worried about saving his own skin, and Darcey was right, a man could have got away. There'd been three in it, Gault, a Seminole, and Brannigan. Jarstad had heard Akins say Gault was dead, and the Seminole didn't look the part. Brannigan neither.

Jarstad looked again and mentally shook his head. He didn't know what he'd expected but certainly not this. He knew Darcey was having second thoughts—well, maybe he was with Darcey. The stolen money was here somewhere, It had to be, but somehow it didn't seem so important as before.

Frobish swore and clutched his arm. The shirt was slit clean and blood welled strong from a deep gouge.

Another bullet hit the rock face below Brannigan and he lifted a hand to his cheek, surprised to find it had come away wet. He shook his head at Sean's anxious look. "Only a scratch," he said and smelled the rankness of his own sweat and unwashed clothing, of dust and the heavy reek of gunpowder. He let go again, missed, and turned at a touch on his back to find Pilar behind him.

"I come to help," she said, "you get me a gun, please?"

Chagro dropped a hand on her shoulder and squeezed it gently. "No, you go on back. We don't need women's help yet. I'll let you know if we do.

You go on back.''

She nodded, and something like stars were in her eyes. "I go," she agreed and retreated, crouching low to keep from revealing herself above the breastworks.

"A fine woman," the Seminole murmured. He held his rifle centered on the belly of a tall Indian and fired. The Comanche jerked violently, lost his grip on his pony's mane, and fell. "A fine girl." The Seminole's smooth, brown face showed no emotion at all, only his eyes held a remote, pained expression.

Frobish had tied his neckerchief around his arm to stop the blood.

"Bad?" Darcey asked.

"No," said Frobish shortly. "See that big fellow? He's come all fancied up, got more paint on him than the rest of 'em put together. What do you make of it?"

"Notice he doesn't get too close," grunted Darcey. "Can't get a shot at him."

"Might as well give up anyhow," retorted Frobish. "Must be fifty redskins out there. How long we goin' to last with that?"

The battle had begun to shift and spread out, dangerously. An oblique shot whined from the rear, from high up on the tumbled rocky mesa above them. In the basin a mule screamed, threshed, and dropped. Carlos and one of his men left their positions quickly to quiet the other stock. There was rifle fire from above, then silence; the marksman was nowhere in sight.

"Settin' ducks again," Akins said through his teeth. "I knew it would happen."

"Get the guard?"

"No, he's still up there but God knows for how long."

Sean said nothing. For some time, his rifle bore had been following a particular target, one that consistently refused to come in closer. A magnificent specimen, impressive in appearance. His skin gleamed copper in the dull light, his chest was broad, his stature huge. Sean studied that figure, steeling himself to the job at hand and forgetting all else.

There was a little wind—from the east. He permitted himself a brief glance at the sky, which had grown even more gray, and lowering clouds gathered heavy on the mountaintops, obscuring the landscape. It would rain soon, already there was moisture in the low-pressing air. His finger tightened on the trigger, loosed again, and he waited.

"See him, Pa?"

"I see him."

Again the finger tightened, again the wait. When the rifle spoke it was almost gently, and the spotted horse reared and came down with a jarring thump, its rider swiveled half off the animal's back with the motion, but most of all from death itself. He had been shot straight through the head. He fell heavily.

The Indians were milling, disorganized, and uncertain. They drew back for some kind of palaver, thought the better of it, scooped up the body of their fallen leader, and all swept off toward the east, in the direction they had come.

## SIXTEEN

"Gone, by God," somebody breathed.

"They'll be back and this time they won't fool around," Brannigan said.

Akins nodded. "That's right. They figured to go home with an easy take to brag about. Make the young squaws sit up and take notice. Carlos says there's not another place as good as this closer than five miles, and he knows this country like the back of his hand. We'd never make it, so we better sit it out right here. Darcey, you was in the Creek rebellion—want to bet what they'll do next?"

"Eat us alive," said Darcey and glanced thoughtfully at Chagro, at Sean. "They lost their head man but that won't stop 'em. They got guns as good as us, they got the numbers. What else? Anybody with any bright ideas better spit 'em out now. There's tonight but that won't last forever."

"A little breathin' spell," growled Frobish and eased his wounded arm. "Guess we're lucky, at that. Not a flash in the pan to some scraps I been in."

"Not over yet," reminded Darcey. "You said it yourself, a breathing spell. We got to think what to do."

Jarstad, long silent, said in an aside to Akins, "Who's the kid?"

"Brannigan's son."

"Well, that was damn good shootin'. Never seen better. Kid's not to blame for whatever his Dad might of done. I like kids," grunted Jarstad and heaved heavily to his feet. He was fifty-three and feeling his years. Legs not as good as they used to be, and sitting too long in one position stiffened a man up and made him hurt all over.

"Mighty fine gun you got there," Akins heard him say a moment later to Sean. Sean was polite, withdrawn—scared, Akins thought, and wary because of Jarstad's nearness to his father. But Jarstad meant no harm, he was what he appeared to be, a big, lumbering farmer, kind, and he liked kids. Never married. He had a heart as big as all outdoors. Akins guessed he was at odds with himself about Brannigan, couldn't quite figure him out. Frobish—Akins didn't know. Frobish would have his measure of blood.

Later Chagro, Sean, and the Seminole sat in a knot apart. "What did he mean about we got tonight?" Sean asked.

"Indians don't like to fight at night," Chagro said. "It goes against their religious principles. They believe the spirits of their dead roam in the dark and fightin' makes 'em unhappy—disturbs 'em. Maybe something to it too, I've known some

187

mighty fine Indians."

The Seminole lay back, his arms beneath his head. The small fires were dying down, the night wind blew cool with its hint of rain, the sky had cleared, and upstairs was a bucket of black sprinkled with a thousand stars. He was to go on watch at midnight. The stock had settled down despite its hunger. They would have to graze tomorrow—but would there be a tomorrow, or only the beginnings of one?

He turned his head and smiled at Sean. He liked kids, too. He liked this one. The gold didn't worry him at all, in fact, it didn't seem to worry Brannigan either. Brannigan was restless and wanted to get away, but he didn't appear to care too much about the gold one way or another. It was the long trip he supposed, the fighting, the loss of life, and the thwarting of plans. The trouble was Chagro Brannigan was no crook. Or in Brannigan's own words, a hell of a crook.

Thirty thousand, ten thousand, or one thousand, you couldn't eat it, couldn't drink it, and it wasn't soft beneath your head. Simple things were all a man needed if he only knew it.

He lay looking up, breathing quietly and evenly, until he could feel himself slip away as he'd done when he was a boy. The murmur of voices went on, the stock moved under the blanket of night, the sweet pungent smell of woodsmoke drifted along the ground. He slept.

"I guess I like bein' here," Sean murmured, "even with the fix we're in. Somehow I don't feel so scared anymore. It's like something good will happen and we'll get out of this. Pa, you never said. What did you do before I found you?"

Brannigan held a small twig in his big palm, he broke it, broke it again, and tossed the pieces away. "Drifted around, fought a lot. No anchor anywhere. Things beginnin' to look different now, fightin' for fightin's sake just not good enough anymore. A man has to grow out of it, I guess. Anyway, I always figured some day I'd get me a little piece of ground in the hills and build a cabin on it, have a place cleared, corrals an' some horses. A lot of good stuff runnin' wild in the hills, all you got to do is outsmart 'em and get a rope around their necks. Could start a fine string that way. Be a good living, out in the open an' free, lookin' over your own acres, what you'd done with your own hands."

He had never spoken of this before and Sean listened to every word as he spoke of it now.

"Sounds like a real good life. I'd like that, I really would. We going to do that?"

"Sure. We'll do it."

Akins presently came over and hunkered beside Chagro. "You could slip away now if you wanted to," he challenged bluntly, "or later. Best later. Be easier then. Or do you figure on stickin'?"

"Don't count on it. I can be miles away from here by morning, which is what you know I damned well set out to do. Why should I hang around with this bunch? I'll swing higher 'n a kite if I stick an' don't plan on letting that happen. Would you? Put yourself in my place. Man, what do you think—that I'm crazy? I've gone too far to turn back now."

"Gone too far not to," Akins commented and gave Chagro a long and thorough glance, "but do what you please. I won't try to stop you but I won't help you either. I take it if you get wind of the uproar this time, you won't be back."

"Cut that out. What are you tryin' to do, make me bust into tears? I thought you knew me better than that."

"Yeah, I thought I did," Akins said coldly and rose to his feet.

Sean looked at his father, then away, thinking how little like him it sounded. Was it for some reason of his own that he, Sean, didn't know about? Instinct told him not to ask, hurt pushed him because he felt suddenly shut out, alienated.

He hesitated. "Are we really goin'?"

His father stared into the dark, his jaw set hard. Overhead there was a rush of wings, an owl on the hunt. "No," Brannigan said. Relief washed over Sean.

Gloom hung heavy over everything. True dawn would break late because the sky was again thickly overcast. There were a few spatters of rain, and wind was beginning to gust fitfully.

The Seminole was at his post, having been briefed before his departure. Brannigan shook Akins awake. "Over here," he said, and the two walked apart. Chagro spoke briskly, explaining.

"The bell," Akins said, "by God, by God! It just might work! It's our only chance an' worth a try. We'll hoist it up on the hillside where it's hidden from below, but we haven't got much time. Let me get the rest of the fellows up. We'll need help, a lot of it—damned thing's heavy. It just might work," he repeated. "You passed up your chance, now you're stuck," Akins said.

Chagro grunted. "You always did have a hell of a time with your goodbyes. Every day is one more step closer to purgatory, but what's the difference? I didn't like what you said."

Akins roused the men, most of whom had not been asleep, and they rose at once, stamping into their boots, hurriedly buckling on guns.

Weems would remain in camp with the women in case of an accident above. A heavy bell could get away from its handlers and become a dangerous weapon.

Frobish, sour natured at best and angered at the summons, returned to his original contention. "Why should we do what Brannigan says? He's a criminal. For all we know, he could be leadin' us into a trap! I don't trust him, not one damn inch—"

"You want to squat here chewin' the rag by yourself, go ahead," Akins snapped furiously. "Your scalp can hang just as high as anybody else's. Otherwise, if you're of a mind to help, get on with it. You know what we got to do and what there is to work with. Bend your muscles, man! We need doin', not talkin'. We can talk later."

It was a herculean task, most of it done by feeling only and groping their way up the steep slope. Moreover, it had begun to rain in earnest and the rocks were slippery. Once Jarstad would have fallen had it not been for an outthrust arm, and he found Brannigan beside him.

Sean's great size and strength stood him in good stead. Once when the jutting point of a boulder impeded progress entirely, the boy climbed up and balanced the unwieldy object until others gained a foothold to hoist it further.

"Cuss the rain," Darcey growled as he sought a better place for his mud-slick boots, "we could have got this thing where it's going before it started."

"No, rain's good." Jarstad heaved, slipped, heaved again, and let out an explosive breath as a bit more height was won. "Injuns don't like to get wet—they're like—like cats that way. Maybe not so many will come."

"There a place up here to put this thing?" Forbish too was grunting from his exertions. "I don't see no place up here big enough to hide a bell. Bell—hell! This is a damn crazy thing to be doin' in the middle of the night."

"I can think of—worse things," Akins panted. "Yeah, there's a place. Seminole found one. We get it there, it's got to be set just right, free enough to echo good when it's hit—"

"If anybody can hit it," Frobish growled.

"I know one that can. Boys, let's rest awhile. We can catch our breath."

"Didn't remember it was so far," somebody said.

"Always farther up than down," said Akins and mopped the wet from his face.

"What if it falls?"

"We got to be sure it don't. Thing like this weighs three hundred pounds. Hate to get hit by it."

Akins sighed again. "Well, we better just watch out that don't happen—keep out of the way below. Shall we move?"

The upward thrust was resumed, Brannigan got his shoulder to it, and shoved, Sean pulled. "Hoist left a bit! All right, just a minute now. Darcey, can you give me a hand here? Hold on to the clapper—outside's slippery. Good—that'll do. She's home like a charm. Now to prop it—"

The job was done, the task completed. It remained only to wait for daybreak and what was sure to come. Men dug out slickers and built up the fires. Pilar, swathed in man's oilskins down to her shoe tops, busied herself over the fires, making coffee, preparing food.

Annabelle humped, miserable as a wet hen on the sidelines, resentfully watching the girl but not offering to help. Weems thrust a cup at her. "Here, be of some use, for God's sake."

"What do you want me to do?"

"Women's work of course!" yelped Jefferson, completely out of patience. She was puckered up about to bawl again and he didn't like that. He eyed her without much hope. "Don't seem you're much good for anything 'cept in bed an' I've had better there, too. Now rustle your hocks—hear? I want me a wife an' helpmeet, not no confounded drone. Get some coffee!"

"All right, Jefferson." To his surprise, she rose obediently and moved to the fire. He stared after her thoughtfully. Might something come of it after all. Looked like all it took was a firm hand.

The rain beat down harder, driven by the risen wind. It slashed into faces and cut like knives. Sean took up his position, but though faint light was beginning to show in the east, it was still too dark to see well enough for a proper aim.

"Needs a steady hand an' good timing for this," Chagro said.

"I know. I think I can do it. It's got to be a steady Bong—Bong—Bong, all spaced out an' scary like. That's what you mean, isn't it?"

"That's it. No matter what happens, keep it going, slow and even. Like Jarstad said, Indians don't like rain, and they're superstitious. It's their superstition we're counting on."

"All right, Pa. Shootin's no chore, it's only if I do it right."

"You'll do it right. We'll beat this business an' have that cabin in the hills yet, you'll see."

"Pa?"

Chagro paused for one more question. "Yeah?"

"We're goin' to leave as soon as this is over?"

"Just as soon. I'll get some hot coffee—warm you up. A lot's riding on you," Chagro added as he turned away, "an' I'm damn proud. I just wanted you to know."

Frobish had been sitting across the way, darkly eyeing Brannigan and the boy, but mostly Chagro. He said to Akins nearby, "This manhunt seems pretty damn lukewarm to me. Turn this place upside down till we find the gold or choke the information out of 'em. We're the law, ain't we? At least you are, or supposed to be. There he sits an' here you sit. Brannigan's one of 'em, that Injun's

194

another. I say iron 'em now! I'd feel a lot safer."

"Why should I?"

"Why should you?" Frobish exploded. "Because he's goin' to bolt out of here, you wait an' see. What you goin' to do, run after him wavin' the handcuffs? Have a cozy little potty chat with him an' tell him he oughtn't to do it?"

Akins said with a dogged persistence, "He'd have got out of here a lot faster if he'd kept going—not once, but twice now. He saved my life back there out of Camargas an' I'm grateful to him for that. His kid pulled us out of the last hole an' is goin' to pull us out of this one, or try to. All right, we don't owe Brannigan nothing but to hang 'im, but all I can say is think it over. Take matters into your own hands, you'll answer to me. That clear? Subject closed."

# SEVENTEEN

They came with the daylight, not so many as before but with deadly determination. There was no triumphant yelling, no fanfare, only the intent to move in, strike viciously, and have the business over and done, the handful of defenders minor obstructions to be swept aside to get at the stock they meant to have.

Brannigan ran back quickly and climbed up to where Sean was positioned in a rock fall above camp. "We're due to see our action, son. Line up but don't let go until the shooting actually starts. We only want the sound to come through the racket, not drown it out, so they can locate it. In a gale like this, nobody can expect the impossible, but do the best you can. Maybe we can put a few more dents in that old bell for posterity."

"I'll sure try." The boy was at least partly sheltered from gunfire but at the complete mercy of the storm. Waves of wind-driven rain tore at him and water roped off the brim of his hat, sluicing down his back all the way into his sodden boots.

It had been raining hard all night and the small, stone-walled enclosure was a sea of mud. Brannigan knelt in the soup, picking targets, pumping shots. He levered the rifle again and again and felt the slam of recoil against his shoulder, the smell of his own gunpowder sharp in his nostrils.

Akins fought beside Chagro and the Seminole, and strung out farther along the rocks, Jarstad, Frobish, and the others laid down a barrage of lead, but none of it was stopping the Indians. Not this time.

Darcey shouted as a big Indian broke and made directly for the barricade, leaped from his horse, and hurled himself inside. Gripping his rifle in horizontal position, Brannigan came up hard with the roll of his shoulders providing added impetus; the man landed heavily, scrambled up, but before he could swing, Brannigan clubbed him to earth with his rifle butt. Another, spilling over the edge, Akins shot in midair. The Seminole wrestled with a third and freeing his gun, fired upward. The Comanche rolled away dead, with arms flung wide.

Brannigan swung, trying to see up to the boy but was knocked sprawling in the mud, losing his grip on the rifle. He gained his footing and drew his '44, whirling to a blood-smeared savage behind him with knife upraised. He shot and saw the Indian's face dissolve into red pulp.

There was a scream from the ledge and the body of the lookout, one of Carlos's men, tumbled over and over, down the hillside in a cascade of rocks and soaked earth. The mule men's steady gunfire battered the Indians' ranks, but the main body of the group was massing for direct attack. A bullet came through the barricade and struck the Seminole with the sound of a stone dropped into deep mud.

"Do you hear it?"

Chagro didn't turn. "Not yet, but we will."

"Count me out," the Seminole said in his soft voice, and died. Then came the tolling of the bell—

Eerie in the rain and buffeting wind, it spoke deep-toned like some sepulchral voice from the depths of the earth, the slow and measured strokes like an omen. Wind lifted the sound, carried it, rolled it, shredded and whipped it away, a death knell from the east, the west, from the earth beneath and the howling, gray sky above.

The defenders' fire had intensified but the Indians froze, stiffly listening. A redskin halted in the act of climbing over the barricade and Brannigan shot him as he clung, shot again at a second poised to leap, missed, and the Comanche tumbled upon him. A knife whipped through Brannigan's clothing, he twisted aside and felt the blade graze his ribs in a flash of fire. He grasped the corded wrist, slippery with blood and rain, and forced it slowly aside.

The red blade wavered and dropped, Brannigan swept up the knife and drove it hilt deep into the man's belly.

But no more were coming. The defenders' gunfire continued, and over and above and beyond it was that hollow reverberation that shook the earth and froze men's minds. The superstitious looked fearfully upward to face their fathers' gods, with only one mighty urge burgeoned in them—to flee the place that was assuredly cursed.

The battle was over, the attack done, with only the final gunshots to speed the Indians on their way, and the sad, prophetic tolling of that unseen bell to follow them—

Akins was squatting on his heels, blood trickling down his temple from a scalp wound. Three of the drovers were dead, and the Seminole. Chagro rose, this one thought blotting out all else in his mind.

"Still smilin'," Akins said. "He died quick."

Chagro didn't answer. Frobish heaved to his feet, rubbing his knees and cursing. Up on the hillside Sean rested his rifle, then wiping the rain from his face, started down gingerly over the rocks. "I'd have shot sooner, only I kept slippin'," he said. "I'm sure sorry I didn't shoot sooner—"

Brannigan looked up at the boy. "You did fine," then suddenly shouted, "Sean—the bell! Everybody watch out—*bell's comin' down!*"

Rain had loosened the earth, gnawing away steadily at the dirt and gravel, small rivulets of water joined to create other, larger rivulets, these eventually dissolving the soil, and all had not noticed that the great weight had begun to slide. Half the hillside had loosened and was coming down with it, tons of earth and rocks.

The boy turned, saw the danger, and leaped aside. Below, the men, shoving the women before them, crowded to the far edge of the enclosure for safety. Frobish stood a fraction of a second too long to watch. The edge of that avalanche hurled a stone twice the size of a man's head, like a missile. It struck Frobish on the already wounded arm with an impact strong enough to knock him from his feet.

Chagro yelled again and started forward but was driven back, the heavy bell bouncing from point to point, striking rocks and clanging wildly as it fell, then gaining momentum to hurtle the enclosure completely and come to rest in the mud at the bottom of the slope. The hillside was bare, one entire end of the enclosure bare as though a giant hand had passed over it and swept it clean, the dead forever buried beneath it.

"There's a job to be done here," Akins said. "His arm's crushed. It's got to come off."

Men spat and shook their heads. "I can do about anything," Jarstad admitted, "but not that. Never was any good at it."

"Well, you know what'll happen. It'll fester up an' kill him. He won't live long with it mangled like that. Darcey—you?"

"No, I'm like Ole here. He'd wind up worse'n he is now."

"Chagro," Akins said, "you've done it before. You're the only one who can. You want to tackle it? It's up to you."

"Anybody got any whiskey?" Chagro said. "Pour him full—an' keep on pourin'. I want him soused. Pickled. And get a fire and a hot knife.

Pilar? Hand me that canteen."

"*Si.*" The girl was white to the lips but she did as she was bidden.

"Anything I can do?" Weems asked unexpectedly.

"Round up all the liquor you can lay your hands on."

"I got a full bottle an' part of another. Been holdin' out—"

"Get them. And anymore you can find. We may need it before we're through. And if you can stop Mrs. Weems screaming—not hurt, is she?"

"No." Weems retreated, his voice risen angrily above the racket. "You figger because you're female, ever'body's got to kowtow. Get this through your head—nobody gives a damn except you make too much noise. I don't know what the hell kind of women you been around, but it ain't my kind. Now stop that caterwaulin' or I'll belt you into the middle of next week!" Chagro felt almost sorry for the man; whatever Weems did was effective, for the screeching ceased.

"Waste of—good whiskey," Frobish gurgled.

"Never mind the talk, just swallow," Akins advised.

"Coffee?" Chagro said gently to Pilar, even in this moment seeing how pretty she was, how steady her hand. "If you can manage coffee, it'll be good. Warm the men up and take their minds off their troubles."

"I think you better save some of that for yourself," she suggested and attempted a smile, "and not coffee. I make, though."

"Hold him down," Chagro instructed, "until the liquor takes effect. And keep pouring." Chagro stood up and looked around. Akins and Darcey already had a fire going, though God knew where they found enough dry material to make it. Pilar placed a can of water on the blaze and set about making a meal. There was no shortage of water now, though it had stopped raining and the sky was beginning to clear.

Sean said, "I guess you got to do this but I guess you don't like it very much. I know I wouldn't. But you're hurt. Your shirt's ripped and you're all bloody."

"Only a scrape. I'll have Pilar look at it when I'm finished here."

The boy stood by doggedly. "Maybe this wouldn't have happened if I'd shot sooner. Maybe the Seminole wouldn't have died."

"You had nothing to do with it, it would have happened anyway. There was an attack an' men die in an attack. It rained and the hill came down."

"Will the bell be any good any more?"

"Sure. Like I said, a few more dents in it. It'll get where it's going."

Sean took a deep breath, trying not to look. "Do you need me, Pa?"

"No, you've done your part an' then some. It's all right, don't worry. Just help where you can, whatever you see to do, or go on over there by the fire if you want. This is going to take awhile."

The boy turned away, then swung at Chagro's call. "You might bring down the Seminole's saddlebag from up in the basin. I remember him sayin' there was a bottle in it."

"Sure, Pa."

Frobish was gray under the shag of beard and he'd lost considerable blood, but he'd make it. He'd make it fine. Darcey brought the knife.

"Hold 'im down," Chagro instructed. "This is goin' to hurt like hell, even though the booze." It took Darcey and Jarstad and Akins, all three.

Carlos was turning the stock out to graze, watering them from a pool at the bottom of the mud slide. He looked upward. There was the rock called *La Escapada*. True. But for some, not for others. The sun was bright and the earth already steaming. He smelled the odors of food.

Some time later, Frobish woke, fighting his way upward through a tunnel of haze and pain. He remembered the rock and being struck down. After that, guzzling whiskey like there was no tomorrow and the drink going through his body to take some of the pain away. But it came back again, double force, and he thought he'd gone down to the pit of hell—then he fainted.

Frobish raised his good hand and encountered nothingness. It jerked him fully awake. Akins was bending over him.

"Where's it at? Did somebody—?"

"Yeah."

"Brannigan?"

"Yeah," Akins said again. He was chewing tobacco, he spat.

Frobish turned his head weakly. "Brannigan gone?" Akins nodded. "An' the girl, an' the kid?"

"Uh-huh. An' you can set your mind at rest. Seminole's dead but before he died, he confessed. He did the killin's. The money's here safe. It'll go back with me."

Frobish marshalled his scattered thoughts. The Seminole. A debt to pay maybe, a favor the Seminole owed? Men paid their debts in this country, and knowing he was on the way out, took the weight off Brannigan's shoulders. But he remembered Gault—big, hulking brute, looked capable of anything. Belligerent and too quick with a gun. Could it be Gault? That would be it, Frobish thought. Not the Seminole. But Gault was gone and couldn't answer for it. Frobish closed his eyes wearily. Maybe some day he'd ask Akins the straight of it—

Still hurt like hell, he was bathed in hurt. The full import of it hit him and his eyes snapped open again. "An arm! How am I s'posed to take care of all the stuff I got to do?"

"You'll find a way."

Forty miles north in the general direction of Texas rode Brannigan, Sean, and Pilar with their canteens full of water, a plentiful supply of food, and with two packhorses following behind. Twilight, the desert's brief twilight, was near, purple shadows flowing down beautifully over the hills. The air was very clear. All day they had been forging toward those hills. Beyond them was the border, east the Gulf of Mexico, westward and for a thousand miles all that empty country where a man could make a home.

"Where are we going?" Pilar asked.

"Who cares? I'll give you a mountaintop."

"That is all right, so long as you are there."

"And if I'm not?"

"I would come after you."

Chagro grinned, watching her expression soften as it always did when he spoke to her. He turned to include the boy but Sean, he saw, was considerably less than happy. It was something he'd been carrying on his mind these forty miles.

"The sacks, Pa, they got tore."

"Tore—how? When'd it happen?"

"I guess up in the basin. I guess it was there."

"What the *hell*—!" Chagro whirled to the packhorse; the canvas bags were flat and flapping. Empty, both of them, and they had been cut, not torn.

Empty! He looked at Sean but the boy wouldn't meet his eyes, at Pilar but the girl shrugged, spreading her hands.

"I do not know," she said, nor did she.

No string of gold coins glittered a path behind them, none in the dust, or on the hard earth. The basin then, or near it, and in Akins's hands now.

Chagro stared thunderously at the kid, then his broad lips curved in a smile, he threw back his head and laughed, deep and free.

"What the hell?" he roared and kneed his horse into motion. Sean and Pilar followed.

Carlos, having recognized the need for diversion, offered to deliver the bell since he and his drovers had many relatives in El Paso where he mistakenly believed the bell was to go. But he took it to Isleta instead, because some of Juarez' men were in Paso mopping up the last of the Frenchmen. Maximilian had been executed and the place was in a Viva Mexico mood but too many soldiers all around. Said Carlos with a shrug, *Que le hace?* What difference? Paso was large, therefore rich, little Isleta poor, now rich—what is better than a rich town to help a poor one?

So the battered old bell, originally intended for Isleta, reached Isleta after all. It hangs in the church and will ring for the christening of young Charlemagne Sean Abinidab Lopez Brannigan on a certain day, this coming May . . .

# SPECTACULAR SERIES

**NAZI INTERROGATOR**                       **(649, $2.95)**
by Raymond F. Toliver
The terror, the fear, the brutal treatment, and mental torture of WWII prisoners are all revealed in this first-hand account of the Luftwaffe's master interrogator.

**THE SGT. #3: BLOODY BUSH**            **(647, $2.25)**
by Gordon Davis
In this third exciting episode, Sgt. C.J. Mahoney is put to his deadliest test when he's assigned to bail out the First Battalion in Normandy's savage Battle of the Hedgerows.

**SHELTER #3: CHAIN GANG KILL**       **(658, $1.95)**
by Paul Ledd
Shelter finds himself "wanted" by a member of the death battalion who double-crossed him seven years before *and* by a fiery wench. Bound by lust, Shelter aims to please; burning with vengeance, he seeks to kill!

**GUNN #3: DEATH'S HEAD TRAIL**       **(648, $1.95)**
by Jory Sherman
When Gunn stops off in Bannack City he finds plenty of gold, girls, and a gunslingin' outlaw who wants it all. With his hands on his holster and his eyes on the sumptuous Angela Larkin, Gunn goes off hot—on his enemy's trail!

*Available wherever paperbacks are sold, or order direct from the Publisher. Send cover price plus 50¢ per copy for mailing and handling to Zebra Books, 21 East 40th Street, New York, N.Y. 10016. DO NOT SEND CASH!*

# A SPECTACULAR NEW ADULT WESTERN SERIES

**SHELTER #1: PRISONER OF REVENGE**       (598, $1.95)
by Paul Ledd

After seven years in prison for a crime he didn't commit, ex-confederate soldier, Shelter Dorsett, was free and plotting his revenge on the "friends" who had used him in their scheme and left him the blame.

**SHELTER #2: HANGING MOON**       (637, $1.95)
by Paul Ledd

In search of a double-crossing death battalion sergeant, Shelter heads across the Arizona territory—with lucious Drusilla, who is pure gold. So is the cargo hidden beneath the wagon's floorboards. And when Shell discovers it, the trip becomes a passage to hell.

**SHELTER #3: CHAIN GANG KILL**       (658, $1.95)
by Paul Ledd

Shelter finds himself "wanted" by a member of the death battalion who double-crossed him seven years before *and* by a fiery wench. Bound by lust, Shelter aims to please; burning with vengeance, he seeks to kill!

**SHELTER #4: CHINA DOLL**       (682, $1.95)
by Paul Ledd

The closer the *Drake* sails to San Francisco, the closer Shelter is to the target of his revenge. Shell thinks he's the only passenger on board, until he discovers the woman hiding below deck whose captivating powers steer him off course.

*Available wherever paperbacks are sold, or order direct from the Publisher. Send cover price plus 50¢ per copy for mailing and handling to Zebra Books, 21 East 40th Street, New York, N.Y. 10016. DO NOT SEND CASH!*